A HIGGLEDY PIGGLEDY GROWING UP

First published in India by HarperCollins *Children's* Books
An imprint of HarperCollins *Publishers* in 2024
4th Floor, Tower A, Building No. 10, DLF Cyber City,
DLF Phase II, Gurugram, Haryana – 122002
www.harpercollins.co.in

2 4 6 8 10 9 7 5 3 1

P-ISBN: 978-93-5699-975-6
E-ISBN: 978-93-5699-684-7

This is a work of fiction and all characters and incidents described in this book are the product of the author's imagination. Any resemblance to actual persons, living or dead, is entirely coincidental.

Cover illustrations: Stuti Sen
Cover design: Stuti Sen and Sanjoli C.

Typeset in 12/17 Aldine401 BT at
Manipal Technologies Limited, Manipal

Printed and bound at Replika Press Pvt. Ltd.

HarperCollinsIn

MIX
Paper | Supporting responsible forestry
FSC™ C016779
FSC
www.fsc.org

A HIGGLEDY PIGGLEDY GROWING UP

POILE SENGUPTA

HarperCollins *Children's Books*

For my family, Abhijit, Alo Anasuya,

Aditya, Anindita, Ashwin, Amaya, Raju,

Pamposh — always my family.

Hi. My name is Neel and I want to tell you how I grew up suddenly in three months. Between Jan and March this year. No, this is not the story of a medical marvel or anything unscientific like that. I am very scientific even though I wanted to be a footballer—world famous like Pele or Rooney—and now I want to write history textbooks. This is because our history textbooks are very, very boring. They are so boring that half the time I wish I could live on some planet which has just been discovered and therefore has no history.

The strange thing about growing up is that it is so unnoticeable, and so higgledy-piggledy. That word, higgledy-piggledy, I learnt from my grandmother. Anyway, about growing up, you never know when it happens till some aunt or uncle you meet after many years, says, "O my! How you've grown! I would never have recognized you if I saw you on the road etc..."

Well, I have grown up now and it is April. I've checked my height against the pencil mark on the wall in my room. No change since January. I have looked into the mirror. My face shows nothing between my nose and my upper lip. You should see the boy next door. Rafi. I am nearly fourteen and Rafi is three-and-a-half years older. He is very tall and already has a thin line under his nose. How the girls run after him. I used to wonder if he drew a line there himself. He is very good in biology, especially in drawing.

Of course, another way to find out about growing up is through your shoes. I seem to need a new pair every term. My mother says every fifteen days, but I think that is an exaggeration. And then, apart from growing taller, or getting a moustache, or finding your toes come out of your shoes, there is one more way to check whether you have grown up. No, my voice has not yet broken…I wish mine would hurry up and break. Why call it breaking though? My voice is not a glass bottle.

So…nothing seems to have changed in me in three months. And, yet, everything around me has. Though I love football, I now want to read history books so that I can one day write a history textbook.

But let me get down to my story.

JANUARY

It all started with our history teacher Mrs D'Souza asking us to write an essay on India's independence struggle. I wrote about Gandhi and Subhas Chandra Bose and Nehru, Abdul Kalam, Rani Kittamma and Rani Jhansi. Mrs D'Souza smiled when she glanced at my sheet. I thought then that I might get an A. After all, I had used all those names of our leaders who had fought for our Independence.

I know now that a smile has many meanings. You see, I did not get an A. In fact, let me be frank and open and noble. What I got for that history essay was a C. Mrs D'Souza told me that history was based on facts, pure facts and could not be "fanciful fiction." Then why did she smile when she looked at my essay? That was a fact, wasn't it? Her smile I mean. And it made me think that…anyway, all that's history now.

By the way, I must tell also you here about my English teacher, Miss Swami. She is very "allergic", her word, to the word "etc." She says she gets an itch on her right hand if she sees an "etc.," in our answers, and it is such an itchy itch that it makes her tear up the whole page. That is why many of us have very thin English homework and classwork notebooks. I have now almost stopped using that word etc., but it creeps in now and then.

I used to think that Miss Swami's allergy was really sort of poetic, and it showed how sensitive she was, but let me assure you that this opinion of mine is all in the past, and will have to be dug up by archaeologists if someone wants to write my biography.

But before I carry on, let me tell you a little about my family. We live in Bengaluru, in a colony on the outskirts of the city. There were seven of us, once, living in the same space, which has a ground floor and a first floor. There is also a terrace right on top, from where you can see other terraces and the tops of other houses and a whole lot of washing lines with clothes wriggling on them. Honestly, you can't imagine how much washing is done in these houses. Ours, too, of course. I must tell you that almost everyone in our colony seems to have a washing machine, but not a dryer. I don't know why. So all the clothes are dried out in the sun. According to my mother, you can tell a lot about a family from the washing on their lines. Hm. There's a lot more to this observation than meets the eye and ear.

My grandfather and grandmother, who were born before India's independence, never climbed up to the first floor or to the terrace of our home. This house, also holds their son, i.e., my father, his wife, i.e., my mother, my uncle, i.e., my father's younger brother, and his niece, i.e., my pesky sister. And of course, my father's son, which is me. I thought I might draw a map of our house for you, but I gave up.

Anyway, to get back to what happened that day, the day I began growing up. It was a Sunday morning when it all started—the ruckus, a crashing and a screaming and a wailing and a shouting. There was so much noise, such a racket that I had to stop tying my shoe laces. I was getting ready to leave for some football practice. I really thought the birds would fall off the tree branches they were lazing on, crows and sparrows and kites, a couple of parrots and maybe a small squirrel chatting with the birds.

Now let me "decode"—my uncle's favourite word—for you what was going on. In other words, let me explain, sound by sound, what the chaos was all about. The wailing sound was from our next door neighbour's house, so was the screaming. The shouting was shared between three or four houses in the near neighbourhood, including ours. The crashing sound, mostly of steel plates and dishes was from our kitchen.

Now the details.

Mr and Mrs Raj, who live next door, are terrified of two things, no, three actually. They are petrified of—1. burglars breaking into their house when they are not in; 2. their son, Rafi, getting a cold; and 3. their son, the same Rafi, being a genius.

"O! O!" Mrs Raj moans over the garden wall whenever she catches sight of my mother. "It ees so veree deefficult to have a breeliant son. You don't know. You are lucky. Your both children are nice but..." At this point, she always has a coughing bout and so my mother murmurs something, usually about the phone ringing, and hurries away.

Now, I must warn you of a curious thing. Mrs Raj is a repeater. No, no. Not in the way students are called repeaters if the poor chaps or chapesses have to stay in the same class for another year. I really don't know whether Mrs Raj was a school repeater, but she is certainly a statement repeater. She makes the same remarks each time she meets some unwary neighbour. These remarks are in the following categories—1. about her son's geniusness 2. about her "nevver" going out of the house except A. to buy "grosseries", B. to buy fish, C. to visit very very "clause" friends, D. to buy clothes, E. to help her "clause" friends to buy clothes, F. to play tambola with them, G.H.I.J.K. etc., to go once a week, "only once a week", for a movie with Mr Raj. "That one Sunday evening is only time when we both go out. Only that one Sunday, we both are not in our house. But…" she goes on not allowing her captive to say anything, "but we do not have the house empty. No no. That one Sunday, Rafi's maths teacher comes for tuition."

Apparently, once long, long ago, an alert hostage listener asked Mrs Raj, "You mean your son teaches a maths tutor?"

"At which point," I heard my mother tell my father, "Mrs Raj laughed so much that she started coughing."

I presume the smart prisoner took her chance and escaped, blessing all coughs and sneezes and catches of breath. I have come to realize that coughs and sneezes, like smiles, have many meanings.

But I must return to the main point. Must focus on what happened that Sunday morning. It all happened because Rafi's maths teacher was out of town, so there could be no tuition for the genius that day. But Mrs Raj could not do without her weekly film. "We two have to go to some cinema hall one day, at least, no? What other kind of outing we have, tell me. All the time work, work, work only. So bad for health, no?"

So, that day, for health reasons, the entire Raj family, all three of them, went for a morning show, not an evening one, a Walt Disney film. And so, that afternoon, Mrs Raj wailed as she came out to broadcast the outrageous fact that burglars had broken into their house.

"Tom and Jerry is good for children, you know," she declared between sniffs. "No bad dancing and what not. Our Rafi, even if he is seventeen years old, is very, very sensiteeve. And who said thieves come in the morning? They only attack in evening or night time, ees it not? Also, we kept all our washed and wet clothes on the line outside, in front and back of the house. So people will think we are inside. But the thieves they were very clever, more cleverer than me..."

Somebody asked timidly, "What did they steal, Mrs Raj?"

Somebody else, a little bolder, said, "They must have taken everything! Cleaned out the house. They had enough time. Did you tell anybody you were going for a movie, Mrs Raj?"

"Nevver," screamed Mrs Raj. "I nevver tell annybody. Not even neighbours. Some thief may be hearing."

From inside their house, Mr Raj shouted in very bad language, which I can't write here. After all, I have a responsibility for the morals of my readers. They were very bad words and Mr Raj has a very loud voice.

"My fish curry," he was yelling. "And all my beer. Those #&%&****..." Those symbols are in the place of the bad words he used.

But what was this about fish curry and beer? Were they his private bad words? A code? It was all very puzzling till Mrs Raj gave out a particularly loud scream. "My feesh curry! Aw! Aw!" she shrieked. "So good for Rafi's brains. And for my hair. And all my cutlets! Even my raita! Aw! Aw! Awww! I hope their stomachs barn! Hope they get aalcers! They never even washed the plates which they used. They have made my Rafi to staarve! What will happen to his genius now?"

From inside their house, Mr Raj was still bawling, "They could have left at least two bottles for me. At least that! A couple of bottles! What kind of fellows are these rascals? No consideration at all. No manners!"

Suddenly, Mrs Raj turned her attention to him. "It is all your fault only. Why you brought so much beer? Then itself I told you. No. No. Everybody will see. So many, many bottles. Thieves also saw...you see now? All your fault. All your fault only."

Of course, Mr Raj did not wait for her to finish her monologue but yelled back using colourful language which I could not hear. My mother called me down for lunch just then. I did want to hear it, but you know mothers…I moved away from my window and went downstairs.

I was surprised to see that we had a visitor for lunch. My mother seemed to have gone next door and invited Rafi to eat with us. He was sitting at the dining table, trying to answer the rain of questions pouring on him courtesy my grandmother, my grandfather, my uncle and my pesky sister. Rafi was also looking very hungry. When the others finally began eating, and there was some amount of silence, Rafi told us what had happened. He spoke very quietly and clearly, I must say.

"This was the first time I can remember when there was nobody in the house; it was totally empty. My mother is terrified of burglars. Today, since we were all going out, she had taken every precaution she knew. She kept a light on, the TV was also playing and there were the clothes left on the line outside. Anybody passing by would assume there was somebody at home. How did the thieves know the house was empty? It's a puzzle."

"They must have seen you all go out together," piped up my sister. The pesky one.

Rafi looked up from his plate with some surprise.

"True," he said, and spoke to my sister as if there was nobody else in the room. "I thought of that too. But you see, we did not go out together. My parents went out first from the front door. I came out through the back door and met them, taking a roundabout route, at the cinema."

"Was it a good film?" asked my grandmother in her kindliest tone.

My uncle butted in with, "Cinema is an excellent medium of communication and has an enormous reach which ought to be better exploited…"

My sister raised her voice and asked Rafi, "How did they get in?"

Actually, I was waiting to ask that question myself but, you know, I'm more polite than my sister. I generally give way to my elders. My pesky sister generally doesn't. And nobody seems to mind, I tell you.

Anyway, Rafi again addressed my sister as if none of us was present, which I considered very rude since he had not answered my grandmother's well-mannered question.

"That is the second mystery of three," Rafi told my sister. "The first one is, how did they know the house was empty? Two, how did they get in since we found no door or window broken. Three, why did they only eat all our lunch stuff and not steal anything."

My father, who had finished eating, said, "I presume all your doors are self-locking."

Rafi nodded and then said, "Except the back door. That is always bolted from the inside. The door has top, middle and floor level bolts. But because I left the house through the back door today, I locked it on the outside with a number lock."

I was about to say something that would puncture his ballooning ego, when my father spoke again. "And you would have made sure that you turned the numbers around," he said.

"O yes. I set them all at zero," was Rafi's reply.

The tedious lunch finally got over. Rafi actually helped my mother, my sister and me to clear the table. Before he left finally, Rafi thanked my mother "for a super lunch", then my father. He bowed to my grandparents and my uncle as if he was a member of a royal family visiting a commoner's home, waved a "see you" to my sister and turned to leave. My mother asked, "Shall I pack some food for your parents?"

"O no please," he replied. "I don't think either of them will eat anything now. By the evening, the storm would have passed."

He left.

He had not said either a "see you" or even a "bye" to me.

What did I care? Actually, that was the first time I had seen Rafi up close. He was in my school, but he was three classes senior to me and I had never really spoken to him. I had decided he was a snob. I felt so angry, listening to all the praise I was forced to hear.

"O! What a polite boy!" my grandmother said. Snort. "So helpful," my mother chimed in.

"A good, sharp brain!" said my grandfather. "And a sturdy appetite. Would be an asset to the armed forces."

"He won't need to wait like me," my uncle moaned, "for a good job." My sister said nothing but she was humming some unidentifiable tune.

So, I went up to the terrace and kicked my football around a bit, till my mother shouted from below that she was getting a headache. I had to stop. How, I thought then, was a chap to come up in life as a world famous historian-footballer if he was not allowed to practice his kicks? Especially when, a few days earlier, I had hit the same flower pot three times in a row.

I remember thinking that Sunday that I would probably have to write my life story as an under-privileged boy growing up within an unkind family that supported only the female offspring and the neighbour's son, and yet became a celebrated traveller as a football wizard and a genius at writing textbooks that made history exciting.

After consulting my diary, irregularly maintained, I remember now that the Wednesday following that Sunday was an exciting day at school. Usually Wednesdays are awful because we have a civics lesson and Hindi grammar, both in the afternoon. The Wednesday yawns in class are like a bad orchestra, especially when the yawns have to be converted very quickly to coughs, sneezes or sighs of great emotion. The last mentioned—the sigh of great emotion—is not always successful. Once, when it was tried by one of the boys, it was so gusty that his book fell off the desk, along with half his sleep heavy head. When the teacher's droning voice stopped abruptly, he woke up and said he had been thinking deeply about the national flag and how it made him feel so tremendously patriotic, that he had to... Unfortunately, it was the Hindi class, not civics. Actually, I've found with my fund of years of experience, that closing one's eye, or translating a yawn into a sigh, as if in profound philosophical thought, never works.

Anyway, that Wednesday, the civics class was taken by an outsider teacher who talked to us about "the nature of democracy" using that morning's newspaper to show us examples of how democracy works and where it has not. The exciting thing was that this teacher was very interested in our opinions! Since she had distributed the day's newspaper to each student in the class, we had a great and rather noisy discussion—about what democracy was and ought to be, and how terribly our country was being run and how bad the roads were and will somebody do something about the garbage. Most of us were saying what we had heard our parents and grandparents grumble about every day, but who cared about that? We were suddenly being told we were citizens of the largest democracy in the world. As my uncle would say in his pompous way, "India also has one of the world's largest group of young people, of first-time voters. In a very few years, you all will be a part of that group of young voters."

I got such a feeling of power when I heard that.

A vote is like a goal going straight into the net! Imagine that!

The teacher told us again and again, "You all have a voice. Your opinions should be heard even now, as you look around and form your views. It is possible your views will change, but remember our Constitution is your rule book. Never, never forget India's Constitution."

Of course, it's all very well for an outsider teacher to say we have a voice that should be heard, and go off. What happened after she left did not feel democratic one bit. Our maths teacher came in and insisted that we get ready for a surprise test. We protested of course but were our voices heard? No, of course not. We were overruled, squashed like lemon pips. We, the voices of the citizens of the largest democracy in the world in terms of our population, we the soon to be first-time voters, we were squashed. Sigh.

Over dinner that night, we had two very interesting discussions. The first was about democracy. I had been telling the family of the outsider teacher who took the civics class that day and how she had spoken to us as citizens of a democracy whose voices should be heard. My uncle was immensely pleased and spouted all the heavy, long words he always used. Yes. I admit it. I've picked up my vocab from him. I have a secret to tell you. I love reading the dictionary, and not just for dirty words.

Focus.

While my uncle was bubbling up with a burst of words about how "the younger generation must never become attuned to the vagaries of our political masters, but must remain eternally vigilant and defiant…etc., etc.," my mother said, "Yes, it is important that young people should know what is happening in our country."

"TO our country," my uncle shouted. "TO our so-called democracy."

My sister had to join in. To show off, of course. She said, "We also had a discussion on democracy in our class. It was really interesting. I was telling Rafi about it. And he said our country is demo-crazy, not a democracy."

There was a loud guffaw from my grandfather. "That's a clever one," he exclaimed. "Democrazy! Good one. I like that boy!"

"Wish I had thought of it," my uncle said, less loudly. "That's a smart kid." "I agree," my grandmother piped in. "He is a smart boy."

My parents, for once, did not join the praise brigade. Instead, my mother said, "I wonder if the police found anything to help them trace those intruders. The police jeep was outside the house for a long time."

My sister did some more showing off. "No, they did not find anything. Not a single fingerprint or anything," she said. "But I forgot to tell you something important that Rafi told me."

My father stopped eating and looked up.

"You remember there were three mysteries about what happened at Rafi's house?" My sister spoke as if we were all in primary school. My father began eating again.

"The first mystery," my sister went on, "was about how these people knew that the house was empty that morning. It never is left empty. Who could have told them?"

"Do they know now?" my mother asked.

"No," my sister replied. "That remains a mystery. But the second puzzle we think has been solved."

"Who's we?" I asked, rather curtly.

"Rafi, of course, and I," she said with immense immodesty. "You see Rafi's mother never remembers the code they have fixed on that number lock. So she has made up a song with the numbers and she sings it out loud. Even when she is in the market. She thinks that any listener will suppose she is singing some silly jingle. People do, you know."

"What an extremely foolish thing to do," my grandfather said. "She is lucky the house was not cleaned up completely much earlier."

"Obviously, this was a test run," my father said. "And that would be the answer to the third mystery. We should all be careful from now on."

"Rafi has reset their number lock," my sister said with such smugness that I wished I could think of something sharp to say to her. But I couldn't think of anything quickly enough.

I've often found that the best put-downers come much, much later, usually in the middle of the night.

The next thing that happened was on a Friday. I remember this clearly because it was Friday the 13th. My sister very loftily announced that she did not believe in all this nonsense about Friday the 13th and that it was all superstition spread by weak minded people. She was saying this while we were eating pakodas and I almost choked. I'm glad I didn't die though. Because then my mother came in with some exciting news.

Actually it was exciting only for me. For the Banjo family, neighbours in A block, it was Friday the 13th in all its awfulness. Before I go on, let me tell you that my sister became very quiet after we got the news and did not talk about "superstitious nonsense" anymore.

My mother told us what had happened. The Banjo family had got a call on the 12th evening to say that Mrs Banjo's father was seriously ill and was in hospital. There was no time to tell anybody, they left in such a hurry that they did not even take their washing off the line outside. Luckily, they found all the clothes still there when they returned on the 13th afternoon. But when they went into the house, they realized to their horror that it had been ransacked. The thieves had broken open cupboards, taken money and jewellery, also the silver cups displayed in the drawing room. These were cups that had been won by Mr and Mrs Banjo for badminton; they used to play mixed doubles, so my mother said.

This was a real burglary.

As soon as I heard what had happened at the Banjo house, I changed my plans. I decided that before I become a historian, I should be a private investigator, a detective. After all, historians are also detectives in a way. They dig really deep and wide into the past and when they have verified what they found, they fit it to the present day. Detectives do that too, don't they?

Of course, the first thing I had to do was to get more information about what had happened and the second thing was to hunt for clues. I found an old diary which I had not used at all. How young and immature I was not to have recorded my life in these pages. I have to depend so much on my memory now.

Anyway, on Saturday morning I decided I would first ask my mother for the details of the Banjo burglary.

My mother had just finished reading the papers and was folding them back neatly for the rest of the family. I remember when I came out into the verandah, where she was, that it was cool, almost cold there. The sun was still a little sleepy and had only half opened its eyes. My mother was muttering crossly to herself, about the state of the nation or the rising cost of living or something, but she was quite ready to answer my questions. She said that she and my father had gone to visit the Banjo family just as the police team was leaving.

"Did the police find any fingerprints?" I asked.

My mother did not know. I whipped out my notebook and wrote "Fingerprints" and added a large question mark.

"Did they find any other clues?" I asked.

My mother said, "We did not talk to the police, you know. We had gone to ask the family if they needed any help. They were very upset of course, but particularly because some rare music cd's had been stolen too. You know how the Banjo family loves music. The children too."

I wasn't much interested in this, I wanted to know about the real stuff that had gone—the expensive things.

"Some of Mrs Bhonjo's jewellery, a little cash, not much and of course all those silver cups they had won. That was cruel, they can never get those back."

I made some notes and then asked my next question. "How did the burglars get in?"

"Ah," my mother said, "that was a bit of carelessness on the family's part. They were in a terrible hurry and seemed to have forgotten to close one of the upper windows. The one that has a convenient tree branch brushing against it."

I scribbled a few words in my notebook. "Upper window. Tree," I wrote.

My mother began to get up. "Actually," she said, "that window is always kept open for ventilation. Of course, since one or the other members of the family is always in the house, that is never a problem. But this time…" That was when my uncle rolled in, singing.

"This time, this time, they were not in," he sang in his horrible voice. "Who could have told the thieves? It wasn't me, it wasn't me, I swear it wasn't me..."

"Oh come on," my mother said irritably. "Don't make a joke of what is actually a crime."

My stupid uncle began singing again. "This time, this time, it is a crime, "I agree, it is a terrible crime..."

He rolled out again, carrying all the newspapers. He did not notice my mother's glare, I did and I quickly got up, thanked her and left. Hurriedly of course. A good detective and an alert son must know when to get away.

As I fled I heard my mother shouting after me..."And for God's sake remember their name is Bhonjo. Not Banjo or Tanjo or anything outlandish like that...You people have no..."

I banged my door shut...no...I shut my door gently so that I did not have to hear anymore.

Of course I know that Banjo is not really their name. And when I talk to my parents, I try hard to call them by their right name. It's just that we children have all got used to calling them Banjo. And there is a reason for that too. You see the sons in the family, there are five of them, have formed a music band. They all seem to be able to sing and play the guitar and drum the drums and make a lot of noise. Anyway, the Banjo boys used to practice their music in their house but the noise was so bad that the neighbours complained. So, the family rented a small shed-like place near the market where the band could have their sessions. There is quite a crowd there on Saturdays and Sundays it seems. That is when I am busy with my football so I haven't been to the Banjo Club. That is what it is called—the Banjo Club. So naturally, the family is called the Banjo family. What else does my mother expect?

Anyway, after I had interviewed my mother, I decided I would go to the Banjo house myself and look for clues. So, after lunch, I took my detective notebook and set out on the trail of those fiendish thieves. How could they have stolen all the silver cups that Mr and Mrs Ban…sorry Mr and Mrs Bhonjo had won at badminton? That was downright cruel. I thought of my own silver cup with my name on it, which I had won when I came third in an inter-school elocution contest. It was displayed in our drawing room along with a black and white photograph of my grandfather with his booted leg on a dead tiger, and next to that is a long, boring line of framed certificates awarded to my sister for being first in class. They are only certificates, not a silver cup.

Anyway, to get back to my narrative, I had almost reached the service lane that led to the Banjo house, when something struck me. Anyone on detective work, must provide themselves with food. One can never tell where the trail may go and how far away that might be. I had taken nothing with me but I remembered there was a fresh lot of apples on the sideboard in the dining room. So, I turned around and ran home. It was a good thing I did, though it did not seem so at that time. I was running so fast that I did not notice Rafi had come out of his house and was walking with great, demoniac strides down the side road. We collided at the junction.

"Hey!" he shouted. "Hold it boy! What's the big hurry?" What did he mean, calling me "boy"?

"I forgot something important," I said, hoping my tone was cold. "I've come to pick it up."

He opened his mouth and I knew he was about to ask me what this important thing was, when, luckily, my sister appeared at our front door and called out to him.

"I have everything ready, Rafi," she said. She sounded excited. "You know what? I even have the old camera I told you about. We can use it, Mum says. Come! Come in."

"Don't worry, I have my phone," Rafi said. He gave me a look that was cousin to a smirk, and walked into my house as if it was his. MY house. I waited at the gate till he was inside.

"Are you coming in too?" my sister asked and without waiting for an answer, left the door open for all the mosquitoes to invade the house.

When I finally went in, I saw Rafi stuffing apples into his pocket and my sister telling my mother about their plans for the afternoon. She sounded as if she was Sherlock Holmes, Hercule Poirot and Harry Potter rolled into an unholy mess.

I abandoned my own mission immediately. There was no use. They even had a camera and a phone. A smartphone! And here I was, with just an old notebook and a blunt pencil. And no apples.

I remember thinking that day that life was really unfair. Especially to those who happen to be older brothers and whose sisters, younger only by a year, think they are unequalled geniuses.

Now of course, I am more mature and feel a little differently. Just a little.

I remember also that dinner that night was all about detection. My sister went on and on describing in great, painful detail how she and that apple gorging ass Rafi found clues and shoeprints and patches of flattened grass around "the target house" as she called it. At one point, my father who rarely speaks at the dining table, asked "Are you sure you were not being watched?"

My sister replied proudly, "O of course we were. In fact, Sirius and Orion came out to help. They were most interested in our methods."

I was about to ask, as if I too was interested, "What methods?" when my uncle butted in, as usual. And as irrelevantly.

"I really like the names of these kids. Sourced from the solar system I understand. What are the rest of the names?"

My sister seemed a little irked. "They are Sirius, Orion, Apollo, Tritan and Vulcan."

This time, I grabbed my chance. "And their only sister is in my class," I said. "Her name is Twinkle."

"Twinkle!" my uncle guffawed. "Twinkle! O by holy Zeus!"

My grandmother started to say something with food in her mouth and choked. All of us, except my grandfather and my uncle, stopped talking and rushed to help, rubbing her back, thumping it gently. My mother gave her a glass of water, and my father said, as he did every time this happened, "Drink the water slowly, a sip at a time, a small sip."

My grandfather began a long speech about the beautiful names his generation was given by their caring, sensitive parents. My father excused himself and left the table.

Detection and its methods were dumped.

I found out later from my mother that the famous camera did not work! But Rafi's phone did, groan.

On the first day of the following week, Mrs D'Souza gave us another rotten assignment. I thought it rotten then, but actually it wasn't. She wanted us to write "a few lines" on what we feel about our Republic Day. "I don't want anything copied from an encyclopedia or someone's old history notes," she said. "I want to know what you as young citizens feel. You may feel nothing, that's alright. But then you have to say why."

I was really feeling grumpy that morning and this made me worse. Republic Day was just a holiday in January and sometimes it rained that morning just as we were all standing, saluting the flag and wondering when we could go home. Even though the 26th is a holiday, we had to go to school. There was a flag hoisting ceremony, some favoured student made a pathetic, patriotic speech, we clapped before it finished and then we mouthed the national anthem.

At first, I remember, I thought I would just write down what I've written here. After all, Mrs D'Souza had said "a few lines". But…somehow, I didn't feel good about doing this even though it was for her who has a false smile. I remember thinking that if it had been Miss Swami's assignment, I would have been so much more enthu. But that was then. Now I know better, of course. What wrong notions we have when we are young!

When I re-read this, I realize I have brought in a whole lot of school stuff here. Actually much of what happened was outside school, in our colony, Berry Enclave. Why Berry? Nobody seems to know. I remember a foreign visitor to our house, asking my father about the curious name. "Was it because this place was once an orchard where berries grew or because some rich British man called Berry owned the area?" he asked. My father only laughed and murmured something about there being no records. This is what I remember.

My uncle has another theory. He thinks that there was an epidemic of beri-beri around here at some point. Who knows? Whatever it is, maybe I can do my PhD on this. I can call my thesis "Berry or Beri-beri—the Great Mystery".

As I thought of all this, it struck me that all good detective books give a description of the scene or scenes of crime.

So, to start with, all the houses in Berry Enclave are built around rectangular parks; there are eight such parks. These parks are where all the colony quarrels start. This is because there are those who want to play cricket there, others, like me, who are ready with their football and a third group who have come with badminton rackets. I almost forgot, there are also small kids who want to play anything at all, hopscotch, marbles, hide and seek or at just being plain nuisances. I have no idea where these kids think they can hide, when there is not even a leaf sprouting anywhere.

Long ago, I remember asking one of these kids, "Where do you hide when you play hide and seek?" The boy looked at me with great pity and said, "We stand on one leg and then we don't move or even breathe so the den thinks we are a tree see, and goes away."

I henceforth called this boy "the Tree Boy".

Back to the description. Each controversial ground where the quarrels start, and end after some grown up butts in, is surrounded by houses, four houses along the inner long side and three houses along the two short sides of the rectangle. The main road runs along the outer long side. Each block of ten houses is named after a letter in the alphabet—the English alphabet—and we have eight blocks from A to H. The whole colony is shaped somewhat like a cross with two main roads running perpendicular to each other. At the junction where they cross, there is a garden, a very square garden with a small round pool in the middle with a fountain at its centre that had stopped working long ago. This pool is grandly called The Lily Pond, whose sullen sheet of water does not allow either flowers or fish or ducks to live in it. Even very mischievous toes of very mischievous small boys and girls avoid this pond. Some swear that there is a bad-tempered ghost living in it. Certainly, any ghost haunting the pond would be bad tempered, or worse.

We live in Block B in one corner of the long side. Rafi's house is next to ours but is on the short side, so our gates are not in the same line. The Banjos live in Block A, opposite our block and exactly opposite our house. Behind our house is a row of shops. Behind Block A is a park, heavily forbidden to children; it is a walker's park and walkers alone are allowed there. Pah!

Our school is at the edge of the colony, behind the walker's park.

So let me tell you what happened when I went to look around the Banjo house with my notebook and, alas, no camera. I took my pocket compass though, a birthday present from my father, but this did not help in any way except to show that our block faced east and Rafi's house had its back to the north. Actually, when you are woken up at the crack of dawn on a summer's day, you don't need a compass of any kind to tell you from where that idiotic sun is grinning at you.

When I reached the Banjo house, it was very quiet and I didn't see anybody around. None of the brothers or the sister, not even their rather big Alsatian Tiny. I have always been a bit scared of that dog. But there was no barking or anything, so I opened the gate quietly, closed it as quietly, and tiptoed towards the backyard. I remembered that the burglars had got in from a back window. But as I made my way, silently along the grass patches, avoiding the gravel path, I saw something that turned my blood to ice. Yes, really. I was as frozen as the winter sun.

There in front of me, in the filtered light of a very leaf crowded tree, was the dog Tiny, growling low in its throat, and standing next to it, with a smile of triumph, was my classmate, the Banjo sister, Twinkle. For half a second, I thought I would turn around and run. Then it struck me that I was doing nothing wrong; I was just paying the family a visit. Being neighbourly. So I cleared my dry throat and muttered, "Oh hi. I came to pay you a visit. Just...just being neighbourly, you know. After..."

She giggled. “After the burglary?” she asked. “I thought so. How sweet of you. So sweet. You want to see the famous window? Come. I’ll show you. Tiny, quiet! He’s my friend from school.”

Tiny did not seem very impressed by this introduction. The massive dog kept growling. I walked alongside Twinkle, on the side away from the beast.

“There!” she said, pointing up with a sort of pride. “See, that’s where they came in from. They jumped from that tree branch to the ledge, then opened the window wide and got in. So simple. We forgot to shut the window. Everyone was wild with Orion, that is his duty. To close the windows. But I was not angry with him. Orion is so sweet. He helps me bring the clothes in when Pachamma does not. So sweet.”

“But that day, you didn’t,” I pointed out.

“Yes. So sweet of you to remember,” she said and moved closer. “You know I think you have a very good memory. You are really something, you know.”

I did not want to be a “something” at all. I wanted to see whether there were any footprints or shoeprints on the ground. I tried to look for them in the fading daylight. But I couldn’t move much because Tiny was still growling.

“Oh!” Twinkle said. “There are no footprints or anything. The police searched also. Somebody watered the place. So silly. Vulcan had done the watering already. He never forgets. He’s like you that way. Anyway, they splashed water everywhere. It was such a mess, so dirty."

The watering was a curious thing to do, I thought. Was it done to wash away footprints and other clues? I wanted to write my thoughts down in my notebook but I didn't dare take the book out in front of her. I had to remember that somebody had come in and watered the backyard when it was already wet. Maybe the burglars themselves had done it for obvious reasons.

"I better be going," I told Twinkle and turned towards the side garden through which we had come to the back. Tiny growled a little louder. "Tiny!" Twinkle said, "Don't. Go and smell the flowers."

Tiny did not move.

"Would you like to come in?" Twinkle asked me as if she was one gracious hostess. "For a cup of tea? Sirius is in there struggling with some essay. But we need not disturb him." She smiled.

"No. No thank you," I stammered. "Have to go. I…" "Oh! Do you have duties too?" she asked.

I grasped the lifeline. "Y...yes. Have to bring the clothes in. Pachamma, she works for us too...she sometimes goes off without… she went off today."

"Oh, how sweet. What about your sister?"

"She sets the table and all that. Look. I better rush home."

Tiny was still at her side, still growling, and not anywhere near the flowers. Twinkle giggled.

"Tiny hates flowers," she said. She moved even closer and whispered, "I'm doing Sirius' duty today, taking Tiny for his walk. He's so lazy. Want to come?"

"No. I have to rush," I said, wondering why she was whispering and why that damn dog would not stop growling. I began to walk as quickly, cautiously as I could, towards the gate. She followed me.

"I saw your sister doing detective work also," she said, this time quite loudly. "She was with that senior…what is his name?"

"Rafi," I said, hoping to get to the gate ASAP.

"Yes, Rafi. They had a camera and all. I saw them from upstairs." She giggled again. "They did not see me. But you know something?" She had caught up with me and now she grabbed the sleeve of my jacket. She was whispering once more.

"Tiny was with me, and he saw them also, but he did not bark at all. Even when they came into the yard from the back gate. You think your sister has a whatever you call it for dogs? Or that Rafi?"

We were nearly at the gate. "I don't know," I gasped.

"I have to go in to get Tiny's leash," she said. "You can wait here and make friends with him. You want to give him a hug?"

I reached the gate, unlatched it and wrenched my jacket sleeve free. I don't know whether I said thank you or bye or anything. I fled.

Suppose her next question was, "Do you want to give me a hug?"

I have heard some senior boys ask that question, in the shadow of the Games room, when they think PT Ma'am is not around.

Phew. I never thought detective work could be so dangerous. Gawd.

I had a very hard time in school the next day, hiding from Twinkle. Fool that I was, then, I had not thought of the consequences of my visit, my first, to the Banjo house. Luckily for me, on that day, all our teachers behaved like royal tyrants and made us do enormous amounts of class work, especially Mrs D'Souza. At lunch time, I sat close to PT Ma'am's chair and talked to her about her sprained ankle. She was very pleased. And of course, she would not let Twinkle come near. PT Ma'am does not like "lunch time chats" between boys and girls. Thank goodness. What a relief it was when I was able to slink back home.

When I reached home, everyone was in the drawing room, except my father. They were listening to my sister, who it seems, had rushed home with a special mission. She had been told at school by some psychologist person, that we should all spend "quality time" with our families. Why I had to be a part of this mission, I had no clue. But in my house, my sister always gets her way. "So," my sister said, after making sure I was captured, "I thought it would be a good idea to play word games."

"Jolly good idea," my uncle shouted and immediately went back to reading the *Financial World*. "Carry on, I'm listening."

My mother said, "Hurry up, Rhea. It will soon be dinner time."

My grandmother piped up, "Don't confuse the child. She has just come back from school."

Before there could be any more baffling remarks from my grandmother or grandfather, my sister said, "Here are two statements. You have to fill in the blank at the end of the second statement."

She cleared her throat. My grandmother looked anxious. She asked, "Are you getting a cold my dear? Do you want…?"

My sister shook her head, then said, "These are the two statements. One. Indira Gandhi was Jawaharlal Nehru's daughter. Two. Jawaharlal Nehru was Indira Gandhi's father's…what? You have to fill in the blank at the end of that statement."

My uncle threw down the paper and shouted, "I've got it! Favourite flower. Her father's favourite flower."

"There's only one blank," said my sister. "You have to give a single word." "Is it rose?" my grandfather asked. "Her father's rose."

"He wore a fresh one every day, you know," my grandmother said. "Used to pluck it himself. A red rose… always a…"

My uncle shouted again. "I know! I know! Her father's home. Home." "Rubbish!" my grandfather growled. "You are out of your mind."

"I know I'm right," my uncle retorted loudly.

"You are a higgledy-piggledy fellow," my grandmother said and then continued with her shrill remarks. "A red rose. Always a red rose. He wore it in his buttonhole, you know."

In the midst of this family hubbub, so normal and everyday in our house, my mother said very quietly, "Name. Jawaharlal Nehru was her father's name."

Nobody heard her except me. Not even my sister. The argument went on into dinner time when my father came in, looking tired.

"Hey!" my uncle yelled. "Can you answer this riddle? I bet you can't."

He repeated the two statements. "You can use only one word," my uncle said grandly. "I know the answer of course. But you try."

"The answer is 'name'," my father said. "Can we have dinner now? I'm really hungry."

"Ah!" my grandfather exclaimed. "I knew he would get it straight away. Name. That's it. Not house. I have two sons. One a genius. The other an idiot."

"But Amma said it earlier," I told them. "Amma has given the answer already."

But nobody paid any attention. Not even my sister who was laying the table, nor my uncle who was in a sulk nor my grandparents who were asking what there was for dinner. Only my father tousled my hair and from the kitchen, my mother gave me a thumbs up.

Was there a teardrop in her eye? Or did I imagine it?

That was the first time that I thought seriously about gender inequality, and how complicated it was. I remember I hugged my mother very tight that day. But I also remember feeling uncomfortable about Twinkle. How was I to behave with her?

I did not like feeling uncomfortable, I don't think anybody does. So I switched to what Twinkle had told me about the burglary, the stuff I was really interested in. Definitely not her efforts to be great friends with me. Why me? I did look into the bathroom mirror to see whether I was looking a bit different, a little more manly perhaps, but I couldn't be sure. Anyway, I did make a few notes afterwards about how the thieves got in etc. Obviously, it was very easy for them, since the upper window was open and there was a very convenient tree branch almost touching the window ledge. The question that nagged me though, was—how did the burglars know there was nobody in the house? Like the Raj family, the Banjos did not ever leave their house completely empty. One of them was always in and then there was Tiny, the dog. It was forever roaming around in the garden, or snoozing in the back porch. I have seen it myself or rather I have heard its famous low growl whenever I happened to go past that back gate. But this time, the Banjos took Tiny with them too, because they did not know how long they would be away.

But how did the burglars know all this? Especially when the clothes were still out in the yard and the Banjos had left a light on in an upstairs room? Who had told the thieves that the house was actually, safely empty?

Another important question for me—how come Tiny did not bark when my sister and Rafi came snooping? Was there something in what that girl Twinkle had said? That either Rafi or my sister had some kind of friendship with the dog?

With all the detective work and the constant vigil against Twinkle, I had quite forgotten the task Mrs D'Souza had given us, to write about what we thought of our democracy, and what we felt about being citizens of a republic. I had wanted to ask my mother for some good ideas, but every time I looked for her, she was either busy, or not at home. I later found that she and my father had been attending several meetings concerning the thefts in the colony. So I had to find ideas on my own. I looked for books that might be of help, but all that I picked out from our book shelves in the drawing room were huge volumes that were heavy to hold and boring to read. Such massive words. Such mile-long sentences. No wonder we all get turned off. Who can be bothered about democracy and civic rights and duties and boring things like that? But I had to write something and not copy from the civics textbook. I knew there would be more stuff online, but I was not allowed to use the computer, without my parents' permission. And anyway, I knew half the class would just do a copy and paste job from the net. I wanted to do something different, and I didn't know what I was searching for. As I sat there on the floor thinking, I heard the tap tapping of my grandmother's walking stick. Oh no, I thought to myself, now she is going to ask me a hundred questions and hand me thousands of bits of advice, including the constant one about how I should be getting up before the sun did.

How wrong I was!

Yes. My grandmother did ask me what I was up to, but when I told her, what she said was quite astonishing. She sat down carefully in her rocking chair and said, "You know you young people cannot understand many things about our history. About India. It was all so higgledy-piggledy. It is not your fault. You were born so much later. You don't know how it was to feel that we were prisoners in our own country. And then Gandhi came to lead us out of our prison."

"Gandhi gave us back our self-respect," I heard my grandfather say from behind me. "We are a great people but we had forgotten that. We allowed ourselves to be looted."

"But," my grandmother cut in quickly, "Gandhi insisted that we should not become violent. We should gain our freedom in a peaceful way."

"I was angry about that," my grandfather said. "I was a college student then and many of my friends and I wanted to…"

"…become heroes…" my grandmother laughed.

My grandfather turned on her in a sort of exasperated and amused way. "And what did you do, madam?" he asked. "Gave away your gold bangles!"

"O I did," my grandmother said, giggling. Suddenly she looked like my sister, there was the same touch of mischief bubbling up in her old, lined face. "I only wished I had more to give. To Gandhi. For freedom."

"Did you ever meet him? I asked. "Meet Gandhiji?"

"I did," my grandfather replied. "I asked my father whether I could go to Delhi and he understood why even before I told him. He gave me the ticket money and patted me on my shoulder. He had never done that before…" My grandfather paused.

"And I gave him my gold bangle then," Grandma said. "That is when I gave it to him."

"You mean you knew each other?" I asked.

"Of course, we did," they answered together, like children chanting the alphabet.

"We were married," Grandma added.

My head whirled. "But you said you were a student Grandpa," I reminded him. "Yes I was," he said. "I was in college in Madras."

"And I was in school," my grandmother chimed in. "Always first in class."

Grandfather ignored that and said, "Anyway, the important thing is I saw Gandhi. It was 1942 and the freedom struggle had spread across the land. Delhi was alive with his name."

My grandpa's aged eyes also came alive as he remembered those far off days. "Gandhi was to address a meeting the day I arrived. I did not even have to ask where it would be. I just followed the crowd. At first, all I could see was a small man, dressed in a dhoti. He didn't look like a hero at all."

"Not one bit like a hero," my grandmother chuckled. "Not handsome, not tall, no big moustache…"

"Yet, when he spoke," my grandfather said softly, "something happened to us. We were all silent, listening and feeling something very deep in our hearts. I can't explain it. I remember that I felt like crying."

"What did he say?" I asked and found to my surprise that my voice had turned soft too.

"He spoke very simply," Grandpa said. "He used words that people use every day. So even though he spoke in Hindustani, I could understand what he said. And in those ordinary words, he reminded us of who we were, that we were sons and daughters of this land, we were not slaves."

"He said," my grandmother added, "that we must ask the British to go. This was Hindustan, our land, our India, and we wanted it back."

"And we did get it back," I said and for some reason, my voice was a bit wobbly.

"And the British, our former rulers, became our friends," Grandpa added.

"And all those small, small kings and queens gave up their thrones," said Grandma. "And decided to be part of this new India with our own national flag, our own, beautiful national anthem... Oh! It was like we were all born again."

"Don't forget out Constitution, our grand rule book," said my grandfather proudly. "We have probably one of the best written Constitutions in the world. And we must all hail that remarkable man Dr Ambedkar for it."

"O, we have to thank so many, many fine men and women," my grandmother continued just as proudly. "People with names and people without."

This statement I could not figure out immediately till I realized that she was saying that apart from great leaders like Sardar Patel, Nehru, Subash Chandra Bose, Maulana Azad, there were thousands of ordinary people who fought for India's freedom. Ordinary, everyday people whose names did not enter our history books.

The thought made my spine tingle. How many of them would have given up their work, left their families, gone to prison, were perhaps injured, even lost their lives! I remembered suddenly that I had read about Jallianwala Bagh in last year's history textbook, about that horrible General Dyer who ordered his men to fire at hundreds of unarmed men, women and children who had gathered for prayers, who were trapped, couldn't escape those cruel bullets. This had actually happened, this was not just a paragraph in a history book, this was something that had happened in my India. If I had been alive then and living in Punjab...Suddenly I hated the British, hated history, hated...

My grandfather seemed to know what I was thinking. He leaned across to me and patted my cheek. "It is always good to forgive our enemies," he said, chuckling. "They become weaponless, you see. What have they to fight us about then?"

I thought of how it must have been for those living under British rule, being treated like servants, slaves in their own country, and then on the midnight of 15th August 1947 to find themselves free. We became Indians, we were owners of our nation, India.

Later, in my room, I thought of my grandparents being married while they were still students, my grandmother still in school.

I remember that lunch that Sunday was rather strange. No, I don't mean the food was strange. There was nothing on the table that wriggled or squawked. Or dived into the gravy, though that would have been fun. Nothing like that happened. Lunch was strange because my parents were not back and my sister and I had to heat the food and lay the table and serve the rest of us. My sister and I managed to do all of it without a fight. Maybe, it was because our uncle kept laughing at us. We teamed up against him, my sister and me. We were allies. For a while at least.

After lunch, I thought I would start writing something for Mrs D'Souza. My grandparents' stories had made me think a lot. Our freedom struggle had suddenly become much more real now; it was not just a few lines and a list of names and dates in our history textbook. I thought how much more we would understand what it was like in those days, what Gandhi was really like, if we could talk to ordinary people, like my grandparents. I was lucky but how many of my classmates had such grandparents? To me, what they said made much more sense than the speeches of leaders. Yes, I know those are important but aren't ordinary people important too? I was thinking all this and trying to get down to write when my sister called me from downstairs. Her voice had that "you better stop whatever you are doing and come down right now" tone about it. There was no use arguing with her. Also, I was getting a bit tired of being patriotic for so long.

I decided to take my football with me just to show my independent spirit and went downstairs. I found my parents were back. The whole family had gathered in the drawing room looking very solemn, even my uncle for once. I was extremely annoyed to find Rafi there too. I sat down, as close to the door as I could, and put my football under my chair with much grunting, so that everybody would know. Nobody said anything to me but I heard my sister give one of her exasperated sighs.

It was a very serious meeting so I have tried to write down all that happened in the same words that my parents used. Even now, when I think of that evening, I feel shivery.

It was my mother who started the conference. "Your father and I have just come back from a meeting of the Residents' Association. It was an emergency meeting." She paused and my father took over. He spoke more seriously than I had expected.

"We were told," he said, "that there is a gang of young people in and around our colony, who are breaking into houses when the residents are out. We know of those in our immediate neighbourhood, but apparently, there have been break-ins in other blocks too. The police feel strongly that these are not professional thieves because sometimes, they do not steal anything but only…"

"…eat up all the food…" my sister said.

My father did not smile. "That's right," he said. "The police are of the opinion that these are young boys and girls, probably from privileged families, who are indulging in these activities, as a kind of..."

"Time pass," my uncle broke in. "For fun. Time pass."

"Well, that's as good a term as any," my father said quietly. "But whatever word we use, it is a highly distressing situation. I would not like to call these youngsters criminals, but they are going the wrong way."

My grandfather who had been listening very intently, rather abruptly asked, "Are they on drugs as well as alcohol?"

"How did you know about the alcohol?" my father asked in a tone of surprise. Rafi looked down at his shoes.

"They drank up all of Rafi's father's beer," Grandpa replied.

It was only then that I remembered how angry Rafi's father had been about his missing beer. I remember thinking how sharp my grandfather was and then, suddenly, I thought of Gandhiji too.

When everyone looked with admiration at my grandfather, my grandmother decided to show that she was no less smart. "What I want to know," she said, "is how these people knew when to break into a house. How did they know when a house was empty? This colony is full of people who stay at home all the time. Those who do go out, have a caretaker or a guard dog or something. Houses are never left empty. Never. I am telling you this gang had, what you might call, an informer, to help them. An informer. A con-spi-ra-tor."

She lengthened out the last word in a whisper, leaning towards my father as if she did not want anyone else to hear. I tried not to laugh but my uncle burst out in a loud guffaw. "O Amma," he shouted. "This is not wartime or your fight against the Brits. There are no informers or conspirators in this case. The gang must be going about with their ears and eyes open, picking up bits of information here and there."

My grandmother puffed up her cheeks. She looked like a ten-year-old refusing to drink her glass of milk. "Stop being higgledy-piggledy. I am talking about just that, somebody must be giving them those bits and pieces of information," she said and sniffed in a haughty way. My grandmother has different sniffs that have different meanings.

There was a small silence after Grandma's haughty sniff; my uncle picked up a newspaper. I thought I could get up and leave at last. Then Rafi cleared his throat and began to speak. "Some of you," he said, "may be wondering why I am here…"

Nobody said anything.

Rafi coughed and without looking at me, began an explanation. "The point is, my parents are now scared of leaving the house empty at any time. They don't even go for those weekly films any more. But they did want to know what happened at the meeting."

"I'm sure they will want to know," my mother said. "Do tell them what happened, and also tell them that the police will be posting additional constables in our area."

My father added, "In the meanwhile, we have all been asked to be alert and report any stranger loitering about. If you do, please do not accost him…"

"…or her…" This from my mother.

"That's right," my father corrected himself. "Him or her. Please do not accost this person on your own. Just report it to the police or tell one of us. No heroics please."

I was to remember this piece of advice from my father much later in a very different way. How words change meaning according to when they are spoken. That day, sitting in our drawing room, my father warning us about heroics seemed to be the usual, parental order. And as always, it was a conference stopper. Other conversations broke out. My sister who knows everything about everything, started telling Rafi that his parents ought not to miss their weekly outing, it was "essential" that they went out, my uncle began arguing with Grandma about the word "informer". My grandmother retorted that her English was a thousand times better than his because she studied it when the British still ruled India.

I picked up my football and left. After that big family meeting, which included a non-family member, I wanted to clear my irritation, and to think about what my parents had said. I hoped that at least a couple of fellows would be around to practice some goal shots. But I hadn't realized how complicated my life was to become for who did I bump into at the gate with her grumpy dog? Yes. The very same.

"Haaiiii," she squealed. "How nice to see you!" The dog growled.

"I did not expect you to be here," she cooed.

I was about to say that since this was my house where I lived with my parents and grandpar…when she put her finger to her lips and came closer.

"Ssh," she growled. Sorry it was the dog that growled. "Ssshh, we must be careful," she whispered, almost killing my ear. "If my brothers see me here they will finish you, they will…they will cut your throat."

"Why?" I asked, also whispering. Stupidly. I should have just walked away. But brains never work till it is too late. Think of Mohammed bin Tughlaq.

Twinkle looked at me in a funny kind of simpering way.

"Because…because...you…" she giggled. The dog let out a dreadful growl and bared its teeth, I think it was at me.

"O Tiny!" she said and giggled again. "You don't have to be so jealous. Do you know..." this time to me, I suppose. "Do you know Tiny is so jealous of you? He is a silly dog, isn't he? Stop it. Stop it now."

Since the dog kept on with its furious sounds, I assumed those last words were to it but it could also have been to the blessed drops of rain that began pelting down.

"O! O! I must run," she shrieked. "They'll murder me if Tiny gets a cold." She gave me another simpering, coy look. "I'm so sorry. I know you would have liked me to stay but…"

The growling dog with its thick coat and its apparent capacity to catch a cold, dragged her away.

I went in and up to my room. I could not get down to any work. I was still shaking a bit with the recent close encounter and I was also thinking of my future. Was my entire life to be about how to dodge this girl and her blasted dog? Was this what it was to be? Avoiding her somehow at school and then finding her lying in wait at my gate?

Lying in wait at the gate.

Lying in wait… At the gate…

And suddenly, in the strange way in which these things happen, I got my idea for the history project.

I would write a poem. And that is what I did.

In 1947, we became independent
Gandhi asked our foreign rulers to go
We were free of the British at last
No more their colony, nor they our foe.

India was free but not yet a nation
Sardar Patel spoke to royalty defenders

He said India should be a democratic republic
So Indians could vote for their own leaders.

In 1950 we became a Sovereign Democratic Republic
Dr Ambedkar wrote for us a brand new Constitution
All Indians, young, old, literate or not
Became the rightful owners of the nation.

We vote for leaders from amongst us
We no longer have kings and queens
Our flag that Jawaharlal Nehru unfurled
Is the most beautiful that I have seen.

In our country, we all have equal rights
This is promised us by our Constitution
We are citizens of an indivisible nation
The colours of our flag is our representation.
Let us sing Jana Gana Mana out loud
Let us salute our flag as it proudly unfurls
No one can demean us or our India
We shall be the best everywhere in the world.

I finished the poem after a lot of crossing outs and getting angry with those miserable rhyming words that don't mean what I want them to mean. Also I was angry with myself for wanting to mix poetry with history. What an idiot I am, I said to myself, quite a number of times. That day, I hoped that Mrs D'Souza wouldn't fling my poor effort into the waste paper basket. She had done it to my homework book before.

I think many historians are like Mrs D'Souza. Look at your history textbook. Every chapter criticizes somebody or the other. Of course, now I have a different opinion about Mrs D'Souza.

Anyway, after I finished the poem, I found there was still some daylight; it had stopped raining, although the sky was quite grey. I decided to go to the F block park and try and get someone to play with. You can guess why I was going so far away. But before that, I had to make sure that it was safe to go out, that she was not hanging around my house with that dog of hers. I went up to the terrace and crouched near the wall. I had to make very sure that I couldn't be seen. Very, very carefully I peeped over the parapet, hoping she wouldn't look up suddenly. I searched the road, and near our gate. There seemed to be no one around. The air was damp and cold. I assumed that anyone sensible would like to stay inside or, of course, kick a ball about in the park. Not walk a dog. But then, I was thinking of sensible people.

I took my football and went down and out of the gate, still as cautiously as I could. The road was empty of any girl or dog.

I walked towards Block F, keeping to the rather watery shadows of dripping trees, my ears open for any whisper of a growl. I reached F block safely and surveyed the park. It had a scruffy look as if people had dragged chairs and tables across the weak grass. But it was free of human beings. Except for a tallish boy, whom I had never seen before. He was leaning against the fence on the far side, and chucking small stones towards the base of a tree. He had a good aim but some of his shots went quite wide.

"Hey!" he called out when he caught sight of me. "Hey! You've saved my life. I thought I would die of boredom… Come on, let's do some serious dribbling with that idle football of yours…"

He talked curiously like a grown up but when we started playing, I found his feet moved like a wizard's. He was so quick I could hardly see the ball, let alone get close to it. He was terrific and I was sweating trying to keep up with him. What I liked about him was that when I did outmanoeuvre him, he patted me and murmured, "nice". He said it so generously that I did not feel he was treating me like a nursery kid. He was so unlike Rafi, quite the opposite, in fact.

Anyway, when it got so dark that we couldn't even see each other's faces, we stopped. I was panting.

"You look really flushed," my new friend said and then, in his strange grown-up way, he went on, "When you get home, don't drink cold water immediately. Wait for a while, and drink something warm." It could almost have been my mother speaking.

"Aren't you going home?" I asked because he had settled himself against the fence again.

"I will. I will in a bit," he said and waved me away with a smile.

I began to walk back home. I was tired but happy too. I had found a really good sort of chap, a real friend.

It was getting awfully dark. I suddenly thought of what my parents had talked about, a gang of hooligans operating around our colony. I began to walk faster and almost bumped into someone walking as fast, but in the opposite direction. To my surprise, it was Pachamma, our maid. "Pachamma!" I said. "You are not at home?"

She gave a small shriek. Then she collected herself and said in a flustered way, that she had got late at one of the houses where she worked, and was now on her way home. She seemed to be in a terrific hurry and also rather nervous. She must have been thinking of that gang too. She murmured something I could not catch, then she crossed me and scuttled away.

My mother was waiting by the front door when I reached home. "It's got really dark," she said. "I think we are in for a storm. Glad you are home."

I had not seen her this worried before. Was it because of that thieving gang? Or the storm that was now announcing itself with a crash of thunder?

It was only much, much later, after I had finished dinner and when I was about to sleep, that I remembered I had not asked my new friend his name. Nor had he asked me mine!

I wondered what that meant. That names were not important?

The next day was the most exciting day in my life. A super exciting day. I went to school in the usual way and almost got late for assembly in the usual way. That day I was late because I forgot it was Monday when we have a drill period. I had to go back home to put on my canvas shoes which were rather dirty and I got a shelling from…but that was not the exciting part.

Classes started. History was in the third period. I handed my poem to Mrs D'Souza. She glanced at my sheet of paper, and smiled. Actually, I did not like that smile. I could not trust it. Not after the last time. So I muttered "It's a poem, Ma'am," and scuttled back to my place.

No. This was not the exciting part of that day either.

The rest of the morning dragged on as usual. I was thanking all the gods for the millionth time that Twinkle could not ask to sit anywhere near me. I was in the last row because I had grown quite tall and she was really short, thank goodness. She sat in the front row, and could not even turn around without the teacher noticing. The dangerous moments for me were always when we had to leave the classroom for recess or lunch. Once or twice, Twinkle had stayed behind, but thank heavens for strict teachers. She is pushed ahead even before I am out of my seat. But that day, what happened was something that had never happened before.

As I came out of class, who should be waiting for me but Mrs D'Souza. She was holding the sheet of paper with my poem and the expression on her face was really strange. It was as if she was struggling with herself not to say something. My heart sank. I thought of that smile of hers that meant many more things than what a smile normally means. I thought of Miss Swami's smile which was a real smile, so I used to think. I had been wrong about that too. That Monday, I looked at Mrs D'Souza and waited. My mouth was quite dry.

"I have just read what you have written," she said, "and I would like you to read it out at the special morning assembly on the 26th when we hoist our flag."

I almost fainted. Was I to read MY poem at the school's flag hoisting ceremony on Republic Day? Was that what Mrs D'Souza was saying? Then she said something more.

"Write out your poem again, as neatly as you can. There is a senior student who has learnt calligraphy. I will ask her to write out your poem using calligraphy, and we can put it up on the notice board. Go now and don't forget to bring me a neatly written copy of the poem tomorrow."

I rushed home after school and told my mother. She hugged me so tightly, I couldn't breathe.

Later, I looked up the word "calligraphy" after asking my mother for the correct spelling. Calligraphy is the art of writing in a kind of decorative way, using a special pen. Like painting, not pictures, but words. It's quite tough, my mother said.

The whole family, including my sister, was very happy when they heard the news. Everyone gave me big hugs, my grandmother cried a bit, my father shook my hand in a very grown up way. But after all this, I began to feel nervous. I remember that, at night, I started imagining everything that could go wrong when I read the poem in front of the whole school. I would stammer or have a very bad bout of coughing or just stand there like a fool, unable to open my mouth. I could almost hear the whole school laughing at me. I began to hate the poem. I wondered why I had ever written the rotten thing. I had been trying to show off to Mrs D'Souza and now I had landed up with something I had never done before. To speak in front of the whole school.

I was in such a fright that I could not do anything. I could not write out the poem neatly, or do my maths homework, or anything. I took my football and went up to the terrace. As I reached the top step, my blood froze. I heard a familiar giggle downstairs at the front door. And a low growl. For a moment, I thought she had heard the news and come to hug me or something. But Mrs D'Souza had said nobody was to be told except my family. "Yours will be a surprise item," she had said.

So why had Twinkle come and what was I to do? I thought feverishly of hiding behind the flower pots or going back to my room and locking the door. Except there was no lock to my door. Only a very stiff top bolt which would take a whole century to push.

Then I heard my mother say, "Thank you for asking, Twinkle dear. But both Neel and Rhea are busy doing their homework. I don't want to disturb them now. Have you finished your homework, dear?"

I heard the giggle, not the words and then the door was shut as firmly as the last full stop in a school essay on "My Favourite Hobbies".

I left my football on the terrace and went down to hug my mother.

She was sitting at the dining table with a lot of books around her, and she was taking notes from one of these. She did not stop when she saw me, so my hug was rather awkward. But then she put down her pen and looked at me and smiled. "Is that girl Twinkle bothering you in school too?" she asked.

"Not much," I muttered. How did my mother get to know these things? "Not all that much," I said again and added, "I can handle it."

"I know you can," my mother said and as she picked up her pen she said something which surprised me a lot. "You'll find that it's not you she is after. I hope you won't feel too bad then."

"Bad?" I said and stared at my mother. "How can I feel bad? I just want her to stop…anyway, who is she after?"

My mother did not reply. She was back at her work and I knew there was no use my asking her any more questions. I left. I do think that women are much smarter about these things than men.

My last thought that night was "O god! What made me write that poem!"

I remember that on the morning of the 24th, I woke up with a high fever. At least, I was quite sure I was seriously sick, probably with a rare form of pneumonia, and that I would be dead before the day ended. But my mother sent me off to school with a thick scarf around my neck, so that everybody merely made fun of me instead of crying over my early death. Mrs D'Souza took one look at me and said, "Now don't you dare fall ill!"

How unkind and cruel the world is. I thought mothers and teachers, at least, would be more caring and request me to stay in bed for about a week. Where?

The next day passed in a daze. I was trying to learn the poem by heart so that, hopefully, I would not stammer or go blank on the big day. But the world does not understand nor does it have any sympathy for the sensitive nature of poets. In the geography period, Mrs Guhan, the teacher pounced on me because apparently I was not paying attention to the lesson. I said of course I was.

"So what is the staple crop in Bangladesh?" she asked. "The Constitution," I answered promptly.

The class laughed so loudly and for so unnecessarily long, that the bell rang before we could visit Bangladesh again. Mrs Guhan was furious with all of us, especially with me, and gave us the whole chapter to learn on our own, with the promise of a test next week.

The class, in their turn, awarded me with the title "the best joker of the year" and Twinkle screamed, "You are the bestest."

It was awful.

I tried to say the poem out aloud in my room that evening, but my voice was shaking so much that I sounded more like a leaf in a big storm than a thirteen and three-quarter-year-old man speaking of his country with pride. I tried to boost my courage by staring at my face in the bathroom mirror, and to tell myself there was a faint black line under my nose. But of course, there was nothing. Finally, I went downstairs, hoping for a sudden earthquake, so I could fall and break all my bones. But all that happened was my finding my grandmother hobbling round the dining table.

"Taking my evening constitution," she announced. That last word hit me in my ribs.

"You are looking sick, my boy. A bit higgledy-piggledy," my grandmother said cheerfully. Before I could tell her that

I was sure I was suffering from malaria and measles and a rare incurable tropical disease, she went on, "Nervous about tomorrow, is it? Don't be. I have a remedy that is very good."

"A medicine?" I asked. Were there such medicines that would make me feel alright about tomorrow?

My grandmother chortled.

"Yes, you can call it a medicine if you like," she said in her quavering voice.

"Is it very bitter?" I asked. Any medicine my grandmother suggested was usually extremely bitter.

She laughed again and laughed so much that she started coughing like Mrs Raj. I rushed into the kitchen to fetch a glass of water. When I got back, my grandmother had stopped coughing and was standing straight and still, holding her walking stick across herself as if it was a sword. Her eyes were glazed and had a faraway look, I almost fainted with fear. Was she in some kind of a fit? Should I call my mother who was not at home? Should I phone the doctor whose number I did not know? In my state of total alarm, I drank up the water meant for my grandmother, at which point, she, i.e., my grandmother came out of whatever she was in, and began laughing all over again.

"Grandma!" I yelled in relief mixed with anger. "What the heck are you up to?"

"Being a statue!" she said, still laughing. "That is what you should imagine when you read your speech."

"Poem," I said.

She paid no attention to the correction, but went on with what she had been saying. "Just pretend that everyone in front of you has turned into a statue. Like in that fairy tale…I forget the name…"

"Cinderella?"

"No, no. The other one with the bad fairy and the needle and everyone frozen for hundreds of years… Oh, I remember now. The dozing beauty."

"You mean 'The Sleeping Beauty'," I said.

"Dozing, sleeping, same thing," my grandmother said. "The thing is that story is so funny. The king may have been eating his lunch and the rice and sambar don't go into his open mouth for hundreds of years. Or the queen is about to sneeze, and the sneeze is locked in her nose or the royal cook is about to…"

"Yes, yes," I said quickly. "I get the idea. I should pretend that everyone in front of me has become a statue in a funny kind of pose. Thank you, Grandma. I'll try that. Thanks."

I ran away even as she was starting off on the royal cook turning into a statue just as he tasted the pepper-hot gravy and burnt his tongue.

Well, I survived the Big Day. No. Not just that. I did very, very well. It was so strange. I had almost not slept the night before, and in the morning, I could not swallow any breakfast.

My mother gave me a hug and said, "Eat just as much as you can."

My father patted me on my back and gave me a thumbs up. My grandfather said, "Think like a soldier, young man." And surprisingly, my sister said, "You'll be great. Just wait and see."

My grandmother pulled me to her as I was leaving and whispered "statue" into my ear. As I reached the front door, my uncle came running down the stairs, his hair all tousled and shouted, "You are already off? Glad I caught you." He thrust a roll of paper into my hands. "Here. Read this. They are notes from a famous Greek philosopher on how to overcome stage fright. At least I think he was Greek but he may have been Roman or…"

"Thanks," I said and "Bye. See you in the evening."

I pushed the sheets into my bag and rushed off before my uncle could start another one of his "vote for me" speeches.

Now that I think of it, I seem to be always running away from some parts of my family.

When I reached school, I found I was quite early, very early actually. I hadn't realized how different school would look at that early hour, about fifteen minutes before the bell rang. The trees seemed to be full of sleepy birds, the sun appeared to be dozing like the princess, and the basketball court looked as if it was away on a holiday. The chowkidar, Bahadur, yawned when he saw me and said, "Itna jaldi kyun?"

I quelled him with a glance and said, "Aaj mera speech hai."

When Bahadur heard that I was giving a speech on Republic Day, he straightened up and gave me a smart salute. I saluted him back and suddenly, I felt much better. Bahadur and I were both citizens of the same great nation, the Republic of India.

The teachers were all bustling in by this time, Mrs D'Souza among them. She gave me a big smile and said, "I'm so glad you are here early. Come. Come inside."

She led me into the building and straight to the staff room. "Here," she said and showed me a chair near the door. "Sit here and I'll call you. Not nervous, are you?"

Before I could say anything, she was off and I sat down wishing I did not have such massive hands and legs.

Sitting inside a staff room is perhaps one of the punishments in hell. But nobody really paid me any attention, not even Miss Swami. I thought I should wave to her but I didn't. Later, I was glad I didn't.

Meanwhile the din outside had grown very loud and I could hear PT Ma'am's whistle blowing almost without a stop. Then the bell rang and, immediately, everything quietened down.

The teachers streamed out and Mrs D'Souza came running in. "What are you doing still sitting here?" she asked angrily to my enormous surprise. "Come on. Come on." She made me stand near the door that led to the school grounds, and said, "Wait till you hear your name being called and then you go up to the mike and read your poem. Understood?"

I nodded. My toes and hands were ice cold. Mrs D'Souza looked at me and without warning, hugged me across the shoulders. "You'll be brilliant," she whispered. Whether it was the hug or the moths and butterflies in my tummy, I stood there in a daze.

The flag went up, the march past went past, the Principal spoke and then my name was called. I don't remember how I walked up to the mike, how I started speaking and when I finished. I didn't recall my grandmother's advice nor how scared I was. I only remember that after I said the last line, there was a moment of silence, and I heard my sister shout, "Neel! That was awesome." Then the clapping started, all around me, like rain.

The teachers were clapping too and smiling. So was the Principal. I moved away from the mike, my legs were feeling rubbery. I didn't know what I was to do, where to stand, but Mrs D'Souza pulled me towards her and there I stood, like a piece of stone. After the ceremony was over and the whole school was being treated to orange juice and chocolate biscuits, the Principal came up to me and shook my hand.

"That was very good, young man," she said. "Keep those ideals intact and who knows, you might become a great national leader, one day."

Then she turned to Mrs D'Souza and said, "We must really get started on that project we were discussing, Mrs D'Souza.

To have a forum where students can express themselves freely, be creative as well as analytical."

I could not hear Mrs D'Souza's reply because she and the Principal walked away and I was accosted by Miss Swami.

"Hi," she said. "I don't seem to have been too good with my poetry lessons. You should have come to me with that poem of yours. It didn't scan at all."

"Scan?" I mumbled through the biscuit crumbs.

"Yes," she said. I hadn't realized how harsh her voice was nor how long her nose. "There was no proper rhythm in your poem. Come and see me, we will rewrite it."

"I will ask Mrs D'Souza about it, Ma'am," I muttered and was actually grateful to Twinkle who rushed up to me, almost pushing Miss Swami out of the way, and began pumping my hand.

"Man, you were awesome," she screamed. "What you said was awesome. So awesome I was crying. Ask Mohini. She stands behind me at assembly. And John. He also noticed. I was crying so much that…"

Miss Swami walked away. And abruptly, Twinkle scooted off.

Then something else happened that sort of took my breath away. One of the Banjo brothers, I think it was Vulcan or maybe Orion, came up to me. "Hey!" he said. "You are super at rhymes and things. Will you write lyrics for us?"

"Us?" I asked. "Who is us?"

"Our club, silly," he replied with a grin. "Our Banjo club." I couldn't think of anything to say but "O".

He continued to say puzzling things. "We thought you could write songs for us, you know," he said. "Songs about love and…"

"Love?" I asked. What did he mean, love?

He grinned again. He really had a very nice smile. "You know about relationships and the boy falling for another girl or the girl dating…haven't you heard about these kinds of songs?"

I shook my head.

"Actually, they are very easy to write," he said.

"You just have to bung in roses and posies and star like eyes and cheeks like mangoes, sorry like…like something or the other."

He stopped and looked at me in an appealing kind of way.

"You are the poet," he said, "not me. You ought to know what to say to a girl."

I didn't want Vulcan or Orion or whoever it was, to know that I hadn't ever said anything like "star-like eyes" to any girl. It is true I didn't have any indication of a moustache yet—he, Vulcan/Orion did, I saw—but why should he know about my not knowing? So I mumbled, "Let me think about it," and turned away.

He gave me a thump on the back. "Do," he said. "Do think about it. And hey, come and hear us sing at the Banjo Club. Saturday evenings. See you there tomorrow yeah?"

Me writing love songs? Me who was having to avoid his sister all the time? Why didn't they ask her to write?

Afterwards, at home, while my sister and I were telling the family all that had happened, and I had given my sister a tight hug, she said that she was scolded for having shouted out like that "on such a solemn occasion".

"But," my sister added, "PT Ma'am was not really angry. Even her whistle was quite soft."

And Miss Swami? Long before I reached home, I had decided NOT to rewrite my poem. And I had also decided that I would use brackets whenever I wanted.

I couldn't sleep that night. I suppose it was all the excitement. I hadn't thought that so many people would like the poem. My class teacher in Std 3, Miss Mary, actually hugged me and said, "You were always good with words, Neel. Maybe you should become a journalist."

"But I want to be a historian, Ma'am," I told her.

"Well, a journalist can also be a historian," she said, "or an artist or a scientist or a sportsperson or an economist...the only thing is they should know the subject really well, and write about it so that their readers find it interesting too."

"Like a teacher," I said and added, "who has to be so many things."

She laughed. It was she, Miss Mary, who had told us to "use our eyes" to look at everything around us, to count the steps we climb to reach our classroom, to look at the cloud shapes in the sky…There was so much she taught us.

But to write a love song? How was I supposed to do that? I didn't even have a crush on any teacher unless it was Miss Swami, but that felt like it was years ago. A love poem?

What did rhyme with "cheeks" anyway?

As I was thinking about all this, not being able to sleep, my mother came in. She had seen the light in my room.

"Not being able to sleep," I explained.

"It must be all the excitement of the day," she said with a smile. "Shall I make you some hot cocoa or something?"

"No," I said, "but can you tell me a story?"

"The kind I told you when you were little?" she asked. "Sometimes," I said, "I feel I am still very little. And quite stupid."

"You'll always be little for me," she assured me. "But not stupid at all. And soon, too soon perhaps,you will become a Big little."

My mother looked suddenly sad.

"Who was bigger?" I asked her the old riddle, hoping it would bring back the smile to her face. "Father Bigger or baby Bigger?"

My mother pretended she didn't know.

"Baby Bigger because she became bigger," I said.

But my mind was on other things. So I stopped the childishness, and as she tucked me under the quilt as if I was still a baby Bigger, I blurted out, "They want me to write love songs."

She stopped and looked at me. "Who?" she asked.

I told her about the conversation with Vulcan/Orion, which I hadn't mentioned to anyone else. My mother sat down at the foot of the bed and asked, "What did you say?"

I told her.

"A good answer," she said with a smile. "It means nothing."

Then she went on, in a serious tone. "Neel," she said. "You are growing up and it is only natural that you will…like or…or have a crush on somebody. It is a very natural thing to happen, and it can be very beautiful. It can sometimes also be terrible. As a young man, you should be careful how you treat a girl, a young woman…"

"I know all about that," I said. "We have sex education classes in school. But what has that to do with writing love songs?"

My mother laughed at last. "Because baby Bigger," she said, "many of these romantic songs talk about love but actually are about the physical part. And some of them are quite vulgar."

I could not quite understand what my mother was trying to say. So I asked her whether it was alright for me to go to the Banjo Club on Saturday evening.

She hesitated, then said, "Yes. Go and see what they do. I am told the boys are very good at their music. Only you must be..."

She stopped. "Your eyes are closing," she said. "Do you want the story or not?" I wanted the story. She began.

I had heard her tell this story many, many times, it was a favourite of mine. I knew every bit of it and so I fell asleep much before she reached the end. I'm sure she must have stopped when she saw that I was fast asleep. She must have put off the light, after giving me a small kiss perhaps, and left the room quietly.

This is the story my mother used to tell me over and over again when I was little. I remember listening to her when she told the same story to my sister. She told us other stories too, but this was the one I never got tired of, especially when I was feeling sick and had fever or something.

"There was once a king who had a very wise man as his minister. One day, the king decided to hold a competition in his kingdom. There was a very big lake in front of the king's palace. In winter, the water of this lake became as cold as ice. The king announced that anyone who stood in the waters of the lake one whole night in winter, would win a thousand gold coins. Many people tried but they could not stand in the freezing water for more than ten minutes.

Then, one evening, a very poor man in rags came to the palace and told the king that he would be able to stand all night in the cold water of the lake.

'But you don't even have proper clothes,' said the king.

'How does that matter?' said the man. 'Whatever I wear will get wet. Besides I am very poor and your reward of one thousand gold coins will help me very much.'

So, the king agreed. The man waded into the lake till the water reached his shoulders and there he stood like a statue. It was a new moon night and so it was dark and very cold. The king's guards who were there to keep watch, stamped their feet and blew on their hands to stay warm. The only bit of light was far away and high up and came from one of the windows of the palace where the baby prince slept.

Hour after hour went by and still the man stood in the lake, not moving, not speaking. When the sun rose slowly in the east, he was still there, waiting for the king to arrive with the thousand gold coins.

When the king finally came to the lakeside with his minister, he found the man, his lips blue, his fingers and toes numb, still standing in the cold lake waters. But he was alive! The king was very pleased. He asked the man, 'How did you stay on in the freezing water all night? Other people have given up after ten minutes.'

The man, who was wishing the sun would hurry up and become warmer, said, 'Your Majesty, there was a small light far away in one of the upper windows of Your Majesty's place. I looked at it all night, kept my mind on it. I think that is what helped me.'

The king flew into a rage.

'Then you cheated,' he yelled. 'That light kept you warm. That is how you managed to stay on. You cheated.'

The king turned to his guards and ordered them to throw the man into jail.

'He's a cheat,' the king shouted. 'A big cheat. He will not get the reward. Never.'

The wise minister watched all this but did not say anything. Next morning, he invited the king to his house for lunch.

'I want to cook a special lunch for you, Your Majesty,' he said. 'When it is ready, I will come myself to take you to my house.'

The king was very pleased. He told the queen that he was going out for lunch and that she should have her meal without him. Then he did all the royal work he had to do and waited for the minister to take him for lunch. The morning went by, the king felt more and more hungry but there was no sign of the minister. Then a messenger came from the minister's house to say that the meal was not yet ready. After another hour went by, the messenger came again with the same news—the food was not yet done. The king was very, very hungry by this time, so he decided to go to the minister's house himself and find out what the problem was.

When he reached the house, he saw a very strange thing. The minister was in the kitchen, standing on the topmost rung of a ladder and looking into a cooking pot which hung from the ceiling. Far below, on the floor, was a wood fire burning brightly.

When the minister saw the king, he came down quickly and said, 'Your Majesty, I'm really sorry. For some reason, the rice has not got cooked at all. It's been hours and hours since I lit the stove and even the water in the cooking pot has not got warm.'

'You fool!' yelled the king. He was now both hungry and angry. 'How do you think the rice will get cooked when it is high up there and the fire is way down here? Don't you have any common sense? How have you become so foolish?'

'But Your Majesty,' said the minister trying to look very foolish, 'yesterday, you told that man who stood in the cold lake all night that the light from a palace window, had kept him warm. That light was high up and far away. It was much further away than my cooking fire here. So, I thought…'

The king did not wait to hear what the minister had thought. He understood what the minister meant. He felt ashamed of himself.

'Set that man free immediately!' he ordered his guards. 'And bring him to me.'

When the man arrived, the king said, 'I am sorry my man. I was really stupid yesterday. How could that small light so far away have kept you warm?'

'The light gave me no warmth,' said the man. 'But I kept my eyes and my mind on it and did not think of the cold water around me.'

'You are a tough man,' the king told him. 'Here is your reward. A thousand gold coins and another thousand because I put you in jail without thinking.'

The king gave a heavy bag of gold coins to the poor man and said, 'I need people like you in my defence force. Will you come and see me in court tomorrow? I shall introduce you to the Head of my army.' The man nodded, he was so overwhelmed he could not speak.

'And now,' the king said, turning to the minister, 'may I get something to eat please?'

The minister had actually got a big banquet all ready for the king and so the minister, his family and His Royal, Rather Stupid Majesty sat down to enjoy a very, very large, rich feast."

I like the story very much because it is clever and funny at the same time. Later, I found the same story, in a book of tales about Emperor Akbar and his wise minister Birbal. When I showed this book to my uncle, he was very angry. He told me that the story was originally about King Krishna Deva Raya of the Vijayanagara Empire and his minister Tenali Raman who was a very wise man.

"I tell you!" my uncle shouted, as if it was my fault. "We in the south are always forgotten. Our history, our heritage, our literature all ignored by those sitting in Delhi. Always! Even our stories are taken away from us. Don't we have wise ministers and foolish kings too?"

I didn't know why my uncle was making such a fuss about which king it was and which minister, so I said nothing to him that day and he went on muttering to himself about the south of India being exploited.

That Saturday, after Republic Day, was very eventful. I remember the morning was quite cold and it looked ready to rain. I thought I heard Twinkle's giggle somewhere outside and that famous low dog growl. I decided to be quite safe and went up to the terrace with my football. I was a sort of hero now and I wanted to feel the heroism inside me. I thought about it while aiming the ball at an already broken flower pot. Had I changed in any way? Was I taller? Had my shoulders become broader? Was there a faint line above my upper lip? Nothing like this had happened. I had looked long at my face in the mirror with all the lights on, but there was nothing under my nose, my face was just the same. My shoulders did not have to squeeze past the door frame nor had my head gone beyond the pencil line on the wall which I had checked only two weeks ago.

So, what did heroism mean to a hero? Who was a hero? The man in the story who stood in the freezing water all night? The minister? Or the king who accepted his mistake? It was all very puzzling. All this thinking made me lose my focus and I broke a couple of flower pots. I was trying to hide the broken bits behind a few plants when I heard a huge commotion downstairs. There were lots of voices talking, shouting, but high above them was the voice of Pachamma, our maid.

I rushed downstairs. The signs of heroism could wait.

There had been another burglary. This time it was in a small house in F block where two old ladies lived. They were sisters and did not go out at all. But that morning, they suddenly decided they would go to the market to buy some nice chocolates to eat after lunch. Our market has a great chocolate shop. When they returned home, they found the back door had been forced open and a lot of things stolen. Apparently, Pachamma was the heroine of the morning, she had called the police.

When I went into the dining room, I found the whole family except my father and my uncle, gathered there, listening to Pachamma. When she saw me, Pachamma said, "You saw me, thambi, no? That day? I was going very fastly to their house only. Every day I go to that house but only evening. Just last two months I started. My uncle's daughter, I only put there, is having baby, okay, so I am going for helping, okay? I am taking dry clothes from outside and put in verandah. I am doing that and cutting few vegetables. That is all. But today I went morning itself. It is going to rain so I said I will put even wet clothes in the verandah now itself. Why they should get more wet? But when I went what I saw? My god, Amma, I …

Just at this moment, my uncle bustled in shouting as usual. "Have you heard? Big news. The Mystery Gang has struck again. Looted antique jewellery, expensive clocks, watches… things that go into pockets, things that don't need a big suspicious looking sack. It was daytime remember. Clever fellows these. They have brains."

He went out whistling. I heard my mother say softly, "I would not call them brainy. They are criminals."

Pachamma took centre stage again. "So, Amma, I went today morning after I am finishing here work, because I am worried about those clothes. Then. Ask what I saw."

Pachamma paused dramatically.

Nobody asked. She went on. "Back door open, okay? Never it is open. Never. Nobody inside. I am calling calling. Nobody. I am so much afraid."

My grandmother asked her whether she had gone into the house.

Pachamma did not seem to like the question. "If I go inside? No, Amma, I am not going inside. Never. Because, I am thinking, this is not seeming okay."

"Okay" is Pachamma's favourite English word.

"Also, you see it was not okay, okay?" Pachamma said, drawing herself up like heroes do in a film.

"The strange point is," my sister said thoughtfully, "how did these thieves know the house was empty? It never is. All of us know the two ladies hardly ever go out. Just like the Raj family and the Banjos." She looked at my mother quickly, but my mum was quiet. This was not the time to correct names.

"So how did the robbers know?" my sister asked again.

Pachamma did not bother to think about something that was dull compared to her screaming and calling the neighbours and "making them" phone the police.

"Then," she went on, "those two ammas came from the market. So shocked they are. Police also came. Asked me so many many questions. I told everything. They asked, 'You went in? You touch anything?' I told 'No, Appa, no'. In TV they are saying, 'You see murder or thievery, just call police. Never touch. Your finger marks will come.'"

She looked at all of us waiting for words of praise. None came. My grandfather turned to go into the drawing room. My grandmother said, "They will not be able to dispose of that jewellery very easily, you know. I used to know those two sisters. The Parsi sisters. Their names are…No. I can't remember. About their jewellery. Each one would be an heirloom, one of a kind."

My mother murmured, "I must go and see them. They must be in such a state of shock."

My sister asked, "May we come too?" I thought she meant Rafi and her but she looked at me.

"Sure," my mother said and smiled.

"I want to come also," my grandmother said. My mother nodded and told her, "If you are not asleep, Amma."

"I never sleep in the afternoon," my grandmother said defiantly. My mother smiled again but did not argue the point.

Much later, I realized that none of us, not even my sister, had asked Pachamma whether she had brought the clothes in after all.

The three of us set out for F block, around tea time. When we were ready to go, we found grandmother fast asleep in her rocking chair.

"Thank goodness," my mother whispered, "let's slip out quick. Since your father is home, we don't have to worry."

As the three of us walked to F block, my mother told us how well she used to know the Doongaji sisters. "We were always visiting them, your grandmother and I, when you two were still very little. They used to load you with cakes and biscuits. Then…"

"Then?" my sister asked.

"They went to England to visit their brother, their only brother. We thought they would take citizenship there and stay on. The house was boarded up, you see, with just a caretaker around. It looked as if they would sell the property once they got their UK citizenship."

"But that didn't happen?" my sister asked.

"No. It didn't," my mother said rather sadly. "We heard there was some kind of quarrel between the sisters and their brother and the ladies came back. And after that they kept to themselves. They somehow did not seem to want visitors."

I wondered whether we should be going there at all now. Suppose they had a dog? Or a nasty caretaker? We reached the house, and rang the bell. I stood close to my mother, ready to protect her. But when the sisters peeped out of a window and saw it was us, they were overjoyed. They threw open the door, hugged my mother, patted my sister and me, and said over and over again, "O thank goodness it is you. And not these inquisitive people who were here, in and out, in and out all afternoon. We almost wished we had a dog. And now what can we give you children? So sorry. We are in such a state, we didn't even eat a proper lunch."

But my mother had come prepared. The three of us had taken turns lugging an enormous picnic basket. I had thought it was a stupid idea to carry food to somebody's house but did not dare say anything to my mother. You never know with mothers. Now I realized my mother had done the right thing. She had brought hot tea in a flask and plenty of sandwiches, cupcakes and samosas. The sisters twittered with delight and hugged my mother and us so many times that I wondered whether we would ever get to eat and hear their story. We finally did and over chutney, egg, and cheese and tomato sandwiches, we heard what had happened that morning.

It was just as we had heard. The two sisters, Miss Persis and Miss Dinaz, suddenly felt like eating chocolates and they decided they would walk to the chocolate shop in the market.

"It was a great adventure for us," they said. "We had not stepped out of the house for more than four years."

The two sisters looked so alike that I realized they were twins. They also spoke together, using the same words; it sounded as if two TV's were on at the same time. It was quite weird.

"So, we got the chocolates, assorted, because we should not get addicted to one taste, you know, and then we walked back home. Then…"

For the first time since we came, I saw their eyes filling with tears. Till then, I had thought they were not much bothered about the theft. Now, they spoke in half sentences, wiping their eyes, the sandwiches forgotten.

"Kitchen window broken…glass shattered…the back door latch forced opened…quite easy to do that…we don't lock it during the day…so much taken…all our precious treasures…"

"Did they break open your cupboards too?" my mother asked.

"No, my dear," was the answer. "We keep everything on display…so we could enjoy them and think of the old times when we went for balls, wearing our finest clothes and…"

Balls? I stopped eating my fifth egg sandwich and was about to ask, when my sister kicked me under the table and whispered, "Dances, silly!".

"But such beautiful heirlooms, should you not have…" my mother said, in a hesitating way.

The sisters suddenly looked angry.

"Kept them in the bank?" they asked. "Is that what you are saying? Tell me what use is that? The police Inspector told us the same thing. You should have kept them in a bank locker. For what? Beautiful things have to be enjoyed. They need air. Do you shut up flowers and perfumes in a bank locker?"

My mother was silent. It was getting dark and the sisters began putting on the lights and thanking us again and again. It was time for us to leave. My mother left a hill of sandwiches for the two sisters, and made the sisters promise they would eat them for dinner, if they didn't feel like cooking.

"Maybe you could have the sandwiches with some hot soup," she suggested. The sisters smiled and promised not to go to bed hungry.

We three walked home in the swiftly gathering dusk. As we went around the park, I thought I saw my new football friend sitting in his usual place, against the park railings. I waved to him but he did not wave back.

I came home and wrote down all that I could remember of the day's happenings. This was a really bad theft. I could not forget the tears in the sisters' eyes and their question, "Do you shut up flowers and perfumes in a bank locker?"

I could not think of the right answer to that question.

I was still thinking of the two elderly sisters as I made my way to the Banjo Club, later that evening. Their life seemed to me to be very empty. They had just themselves and Pachamma. Did they miss their dances, their friends, their brother with whom they had quarrelled? I remembered how, just as we reached home, my sister gave me a quick hug before running into the house.

Now, suddenly, I understood what she was telling me.

The music from the Banjo Club was so loud that I forgot all about the Doongaji sisters and my own sister, as I tried to get into the shed. There was a huge crowd jostling about, a lot of lights and music that drowned my brain. Towards the back of the shed, away from the entrance, I saw the Banjo brothers, all five of them, standing in a sort of semicircle, on a small platform. Two of them were holding guitars, one was thumping on a keyboard, another was banging on drums and one of them was singing. I wedged myself between two fellows who were shaking their heads and shoulders to the thunderous sounds. Then I saw Twinkle, sitting near the singer, clapping her hands vigorously. That dratted dog was there too, but he had been muzzled so he could not bark. He may have been able to growl though, and I decided I should stay as hidden as possible. You never know with dogs.

As I squeezed my way to the side and behind a tallish boy, the music suddenly stopped and I heard one of the Banjo brothers announce my name. He spoke my name. I was so taken aback that I stood where I was, frozen.

The Banjo brother said, "Friends, I am pleased to announce that I have just seen a very important member of our colony enter. He is Neel, a poet and a songwriter. He will soon be writing lyrics for us."

Then he pointed to me and shouted, "Come on, Neel! Come up here. Fellows, put your hands together for Neel."

A huge number of hands pushed me towards the platform. There was a terrible lot of clapping and the yelling of my name. As I stumbled up on to the platform, each of the brothers came up to me and shook my hand with great solemnity. The brother who had caught sight of me, don't ask me how, said, "So, Neel, when will you give us your first masterpiece?"

What was I to say? What masterpiece?

"Give me a little time," I mumbled. I was about to say that I had not promised anything anyway, when suddenly, the music started off again, to the words, "Give me a little time, he says, Give me a little time, a little, a little, a little time."

From the corner of my eye, I saw Twinkle getting up and making her way towards me. I jumped off the platform and shoved and pushed my way through the swaying, clapping crowd and out into the fresh air and a small amount of silence. My mind was in a whirl. How could the Banjo boy, probably it was Vulcan, announce that I would be writing songs for them? I had not said I would. Now he, all of them, had pushed me into a corner. If I didn't write something, it would look bad, very bad. Everyone would say I had broken my promise. But what was I to write?

The market was full of people going in and out of shops. I could not think straight with all the chatter and clutter. I was also afraid Twinkle would suddenly come out of the club. I began to walk very fast towards home. The noise from the Banjo Club became fainter, it was quite dark now, and the air was cold. There were very few people on the road to our house, in fact, there was only one man sauntering down. I could smell his cigarette. It was my uncle.

He was walking so slowly, that I caught up with him quite easily.

"What boy!" he said without even looking at me, "you were at the Banjo Club, is it? Be careful who you talk to there. Some rough customers get in."

I suddenly felt like telling my uncle what had happened in school, and then, about the few minutes in the Club. He listened to me in silence, then he said, "Ah well! That boy did something really smart!"

"What do you mean 'smart'?" I asked, I was so angry, I started shouting. "You think it was smart making out that I had promised something that I had not? In front of a whole bunch of people?"

"Hey, don't get so agitated," he said, "Calm down."

My uncle telling me not to get agitated, to calm down. I would have laughed if I had not been so angry.

He stopped, threw away the cigarette end, and turned to me. "Look, Neel," he said. "I used the word 'smart'. I did not say it was right or correct. What had you said when they first asked you in school?"

"I said I would think about it, something like that," I mumbled.

"You did not say 'no', right?" my uncle asked. "So they decided that you were just playing a little, well, hard to get, and you needed a push. So that's what they did today."

"You mean I should have said 'no' that day itself?" I asked, bewildered by all this.

"Would you have been able to," he countered. "To say 'no'?" I didn't know what to say. I kept quiet.

We walked on.

"This is how business deals are struck," my uncle went on. "When there is no clear refusal, the business man makes a smart move and traps the other party into doing what the business man wants. The other party was, perhaps, only being polite in not saying 'no' straightaway."

"So now, the other party, in this case, me, am trapped," I said feeling wretched. My uncle did not say anything and we walked on.

"And now what am I to do?" I wailed. "I know nothing about this girl boy stuff."

We had reached home. My uncle stopped at the gate, and said, "Of course you know about it. Isn't that girl chasing you all the time?"

Then he opened the gate, walked in and rang the bell.

I went in too, feeling like a detective forced into hiding by crooks who had framed him. I have read a lot of books where this happens. Now I had been framed too, in a different way. I would have to hide not just from Twinkle, but from three of her brothers who were still in school.

The next morning, a Sunday, my father told us at breakfast time, that there was to be an emergency meeting of the Residents' Association in the Committee Hall. The new Inspector of Police for Crime, Mr Khan, would be coming for the meeting. "And I have invited him home for lunch," my father added. "I don't think I have told you that he and I were in school together, he was my junior. He has just been transferred to this area. He would like to talk to you, Neel and Rhea. I have also asked Rafi to be here. He can't be at the meeting because he has his tuition and you two have to take care of your grandparents. But I think Aman, Mr Khan, would like to talk to the three of you and get your perspective on these incidents."

Our perspective. That sounded very important. But did we need to have Rafi around too? I did not like that at all.

The Inspector was a tall man and looked very grand in his uniform. He was not one bit stuffy. There was something about him that made even my uncle behave well and speak only when spoken to. The Inspector did not talk about the thefts or the morning's meeting till we had finished lunch. Then, when we were all in the drawing room with my grandmother in her rocking chair, he began. "You young people know what has been happening in your colony. My predecessor believed that it is a gang of youngsters who are operating here. I agree with her. There is a certain kind of recklessness, even a sense of mischief around these crimes."

"Could you please explain that, Sir?" asked Rafi, also on his best behaviour.

"Well, take what happened at your place," the Inspector said. "Nothing was stolen but all the food was eaten up. And the beer consumed. I am yet to hear of a gang of professional thieves having a party like that after breaking into a house."

"It may have been a test run," said Rafi.

The Inspector looked at him sharply but when he spoke, his words were mild. "Quite possible," he said. "But in the next incident, the gang certainly had their plans worked out. They did a very thorough job there. When we got to the Bhonjo house, we found everything as the thieves had left it, the family had not tried to tidy up the place. So, we saw desk drawers pulled out, cupboards forced open, the wine store ransacked. A couple of gang members also seem to have a taste for classical western music. Some very rare music was also stolen. Again, very unusual."

My grandmother suddenly piped up and addressed the Inspector. "I am telling you my boy," she said, "this group of hooligans has an accomplice who helps them with information. Otherwise, how did they know the house was empty? This is a colony of home sitters. There is always somebody in the house all the time."

The Inspector smiled. "You are right, Ma," he said. "There must be somebody who does not get their own hands dirty but certainly passes on information and takes a commission. Yes. We are looking at that angle also. And that is why, I wanted to talk to you, young people. As I said earlier, we are fairly certain that most of these gang members are not professionals. Many of them may be poor but the brains, the leaders, are most certainly youngsters from privileged families. Like you."

The Inspector paused. I heard my sister gasp. Mr Khan went on, "Yes. It is difficult to accept I know. But thieves are not always from poorer families. Many habitual burglars steal because they are jobless, they have families to feed."

"And these youngsters?" my mother asked. I could make out that she was very disturbed.

"The youngsters are a different lot," the Inspector said. "Some of them may be from poorer families, who see their elders struggling to make ends meet. These children are easily led into schemes that promise them quick money. But I think the leaders of these gangs lead them astray. The rich ones usually have a great deal of charm, of charisma. Many of them do it as a kind of pastime, because they are bored."

"But stealing is wrong!" my mother cried. "It's a crime!"

"Yes. It is," said the Inspector quietly. "But some of these rich youngsters don't see it that way. They have been spoilt by too much money and not enough attention from their parents."

"Or the wrong kind of attention," my mother said. "The parents giving them rich gifts and not their time or affection."

The Inspector nodded in agreement. Then he said, "It is this type of youngster that I have a problem with. They can do so much good. Instead, they lead the genuinely deprived boys into all kinds of wrong ways. Their victims, that is what

I would call them, they want to live well, eat well. They see others swimming in wealth. Why shouldn't they have it too? Such discontent is dangerous, you know. So dangerous..." The Inspector trailed off.

There was a small silence, then my sister said, "You talked about this...this leader sort of person being charismatic. Does that mean he could or she could influence these discontented people to a...a...life of crime?"

It was Rafi who answered. "Of course," he said as if he was a great psychologist or a top police officer. "Of course, he or she can. That's how they control other people, get them to break into homes, get the information they want. Just by talking, being charming."

The Inspector gave Rafi another of his sharp looks. "You are right," he said. "Some people have a great talent with words. They can make out the way others think, the values they hold, they can argue away any sense of ethics, of what is right and what is wrong. Apart from this, such people can gather information without the other person even being aware that they are saying things they ought not to."

"People talk too much," my grandfather said suddenly. "Aman, I think you should advise all residents to lock their tongues."

"Then they won't have to lock up their things," my grandmother cackled.

In the laughter that followed, the Inspector looked at us, at Rafi, my sister and me. "You must keep a sharp look out for anyone behaving suspiciously or a stranger hanging around apparently without anything better to do. Any questions?"

When none of us spoke, he got up, thanked us all, especially my mother for the "excellent meal" and as he reached the door, he turned to my father saying, "Was I rather rude about that pesky dog at this morning's meeting?"

My father laughed. "Not at all," he said. "Many of us were very glad you got that girl to remove the dog."

"I was glad the rest of the family jumped up and took the dog away," the Inspector commented. "Funny that the family did not realize till I pointed it out, that the dog was being a nuisance. But I suppose they've just got used to its growling. The boys looked a fine bunch."

"Good musicians, I believe," said my father, "I don't know much about their type of music but they are all very polite when you meet them. So are the parents. Extremely pleasant to talk to, though, generally, they keep to themselves."

"Unlike the dog," said the Inspector drily. How I liked him for disliking that stupid dog.

"I quite liked that other young man too," the Inspector went on. "The one who was there on his own and spoke as if he was fifty years old, not fifteen or sixteen."

"I haven't seen that boy before," my father started to say, when I burst in. I couldn't help it. "He's my friend," I said. "At least, we have played a game of football together."

"Just the two of you?" the Inspector asked.

"It was a…a…we were sort of practising," I stammered. "At least I was. He was very, very good. I learnt quite a lot about dribbling."

"What's his name?" my uncle asked. Just like him to say something inconvenient. I started stammering again but the Inspector was there to help me out.

"One doesn't ask irrelevant questions when one is in charge of a football," he said smiling. "The young man's name is Ari, short for Arvind, and he moved to this colony about six months ago."

I was so astounded that without thinking, like my uncle, I shouted, "Wow! How did you find all that out?"

My father frowned at me and my uncle started a rebuke but the Inspector patted me on my shoulder. "I was not spellbound by a football at the time," he said. "Nor was he."

After the Inspector left and the others were still talking in the drawing room, I decided to take my football and try to meet my new football friend. Suddenly, I felt that football was what would make me famous. Not poetry. I could of course be a great footballer and a poet. But when the Inspector had spoken of being spellbound by a football, I knew exactly what he meant. I could not see any girl or dog from the terrace, even so, I decided to be wise and go out through the back door. Pachamma was in the kitchen so I asked her to bolt the door after me and went out, hoping I would not hear that dratted low growl anywhere. There was no growl to be heard, but I bumped into the Tree Boy at the end of our row of houses. He had turned the corner at great speed, looking behind him rather than forward, so of course, he knocked me and my football down and the three of us got all tangled up, and fell down in a heap. The Tree Boy said "sorry" a hundred times as we both picked ourselves up and I saved my football from rolling into the gutter. "I am really sorry," said the Tree Boy about the hundred and two-eth time. "I should not have bumped into a poet," he said. "My grandfather says we should treat teachers and poets with great respect. Also, policemen. And PT Ma'am."

"PT Ma'am, certainly," I agreed. "The others too I suppose. Don't know about poets though. But why are you looking over your shoulder the whole time?"

"O nothing," he said, then, "actually I can tell you because you are such a great poet. I am detecting."

"Detecting?" I asked. I was astounded.

"Yes," he replied. "I'm going to be a spy, you see. I spoke to the Inspector today when he was going to the meeting. I told him that when I was a small boy, I was the best in hide and seek in the colony. He said that playing hide and seek was very good training for spyhood. So I am spying."

"You said detecting," I reminded him.

"Same thing," he said. "But listen great poet. I can hear the suspect coming this way. I have to run. If he asks, say you have not seen me. Promise. Cross your heart."

I crossed my heart but he had already disappeared.

Who was the suspect, I wondered. Was there one at all? Then as I walked on, who should appear at the corner, huffing and puffing and very red in the face, but Rafi.

"Ay," he called out in his always rude way, "have you seen a pest around? A totally disgusting pest?"

"Lots of cockroaches around," I said. "No flies though. Too cold for them."

"I meant a pest of a boy," Rafi said through gritted teeth. This "gritted teeth" phrase is a common expression in detective books. But in practice, it is not easy to do. Speak through gritted teeth, I mean.

"A boy?" I asked, as if I had never heard of the species. "I've seen a tree," I said quite truthfully, "But a boy, I don't actually remember."

Rafi walked away muttering about pesky, dratted creatures spying on him, peering through windows, squeezing into hedges as he went by. I waited to hear what he had to say about me, but he had gone too far away by then.

The sky looked down at me, smiling.

When I reached F block I saw my football friend sitting in his usual place, chucking stones across the ground in his usual way. He gave me a big grin. "I hoped you would come," he called out. "And you don't have to be anxious about that damsel with the dog. She has been grounded and the dog as well."

I stared at him. "How did you know about that…that girl?" I asked. He laughed. "I have my methods," he said. "Like Sherlock Holmes." "Well, I know your name now," I boasted.

"Ah! The smart Inspector," he said taking my football and placing it on the ground. "Come on, Neel. Let's play."

Neel? Who could have told him my name? But there was no time to ask him. He was already off like the wind, my football looking as if it was glued to his foot. After that, I could only think of my own foot driving the ball as Ari did, curving it as if it was made of wet clay, firing it as if it was a bullet. We played till it was too dark to see much and then we stopped. Ari still looked fresh, I was sweating and hot.

"Don't rush off and gulp down glasses of cold water," he warned me. "Come, sit here a bit and cool off."

He made place for me on the low parapet wall and I sat next to him, feeling tired and happy. How lucky I was, I thought, to have found a friend like him. Then, I remembered our visit to the Doongaji house and I told Ari of the two sisters and how sad they were about the loss of their treasures. He was quiet. What could he have said anyway? Then I asked, "Didn't you see us? I saw you sitting here, and I waved."

"Oh did you?" Ari spoke as if his mind was somewhere else. "I do apologize. I can be rather absent-minded at times."

That night, I just could not sleep. There were so many questions buzzing around in my head. Why was the Tree Boy spying on Rafi? The Tree Boy was the same chap who used to play hide and seek in our park years ago. He would pretend to be a tree, and his play fellows were so dumb, they actually believed him. But that day I wondered whether the Tree Boy had this thing that the Inspector talked about. Charisma. The word sounded like a disease to me, like asthma. Was the Tree Boy able to fool people? Make them believe things that were not true? Anyway, I realized that the Tree Boy was in my school, probably a student of Class 5 or 6. Why was he spying on Rafi? Had he found out something? Was it possible that people we knew were part of a gang of thieves? Or perhaps were helping a gang of thieves with information? Such a person would be brainy, the Inspector had said and have charisma. Did Rafi have it? Charisma? Rafi? Why did the Inspector look at him so sharply? Why did my sister ask that question in such a troubled way?

Too many questions. Far too many. They buzzed around me like mosquitoes. I didn't want my mother coming in to ask why I was awake. I knew she was very disturbed about the Inspector saying that these thieves were probably young, perhaps teenagers. It was much easier to think of criminals as rough men who spit on the streets and whom we may never have to meet. But young people from families like ours? A very, very uncomfortable thought. I tossed and turned in the dark, not able to stop thinking these difficult thoughts. Then I remembered the Inspector chucking Twinkle and her dog out of the meeting. I slept then.

The day after this, a Monday, the Principal made a surprise announcement at morning assembly. She said that she and the teachers had decided to have a new notice board in the entrance hall of the school. "This board is for you, dear students," she said, "for you to express your views and opinions, to display your creativity, to give us your perspective. Your class teacher will explain how we propose to start and maintain this new venture. Please do help us to make it an exciting journey together. Thank you."

She was about to move away when Miss Swami came up to her, with a smile showing all her teeth, and whispered something. The Principal spoke into the mike again.

"Miss Swami will be in overall charge of the board," she said. "She has reminded me that this first time, we want you to submit something humorous to start us off. It could be a small article or a poem and less than a hundred-and-fifty words. Please submit your entries by Wednesday, the 31st, so that on Monday, the first day of next week, we will have the wall paper, your wall paper, on display. Anything else, Miss Swami?"

Miss Swami shook her head accompanied by another large, false smile. PT Ma'am blew her whistle. We all picked up our bags and began to shuffle forward. Assembly was over.

Our class teacher, Mrs Guhan, told us more about the special notice board. "As Madam Principal said, it is a place where you can give your opinion about what is happening around you. Every two weeks, a new theme would be announced and you can write what you feel. I will hand over your pieces to Miss Swami who will then arrange them on the board."

My heart sank. Miss Swami would never take anything I wrote. Even if I were to write the English alphabet in my best handwriting, she would say, "It doesn't scan, you know. You have not paid attention during my poetry lessons."

Someone asked Mrs Guhan, "Can I write whatever I feel? Nobody will punish me?"

"Of course not!" Mrs Guhan replied. "That is the whole point of this project. We want to know what you feel about things like the school curriculum, the environment, national politics etc. But remember, nothing is to be personal and no bad language is to be used. Please write your name and your class at the bottom of the sheet, and please write legibly, in your best handwriting please. Now, get ready for the quiz on the Bangladesh chapter."

Mrs Guhan, our class teacher also teaches us geography. She has very sharp eyes especially for paper pellets and travelling notes, and very particularly for those who like to take naps in class. There is absolutely no point in telling her that one was not sleeping but was only in deep thought. "Then come up here," she says, "and tell the class what your profound thoughts are. I am sure we shall all benefit from your wisdom."

Of course, we stammer, and some girls start crying and finally, Mrs Guhan sends back Ms or Mr Rip Van Winkle to their places with a stern warning.

That day, when I went down for the small break, wondering how I was to avoid Twinkle, I was saved by the very person I wanted to talk to, the Tree Boy. "Hey, great poet," he called out and pulled at my sleeve. Then he hissed into my ear. "Meet me tomorrow behind the Games room at lunch break, at precisely forty-one minutes past twelve noon. Be sure to be there. I shall say this only once more. Tomorrow. At sharp 12.41pm." Then he was gone. Between Twinkle and the Tree Boy, my poor ear had begun to feel like a train tunnel. But at least I did not have to make any plans on how to avoid Twinkle during the lunch break the next day. That day, luckily for me, she had taken herself off somewhere. So lunch time was quiet too.

At forty-two minutes past twelve, the next day, I sauntered towards the Games room. I wasn't going to rush just because I was a bit late. Besides, the GR was out of bounds for us and I was a bit nervous. But at lunch time, PT Ma'am was usually too busy separating boys from girls and checking for unwary jaws chewing gum, to look at this part of the grounds. The Tree Boy was sitting on a flat stone with a friend whose nose twitched with fear all the five minutes I was there. Every ten seconds, this boy hoarsely whispered, "PT Ma'am, PT Ma'am." The Tree Boy paid no attention. He turned towards me, his eyes bulging because his mouth was crammed with food. Through a small rain of roti and potato curry, he said, "Your neighbour. Keep a strict eye on him. What is he up to? Why does he sneak out of his own house? Sometimes through the back door. Why does he suddenly hide behind someone's gate? Why does he choose back alleys instead of…?"

At this point there was a sudden, piercing whistle and all three of us jumped. The Tree Boy mightily swallowed the last of his roti and potato curry, wiped his mouth in a totally ineffective way and ran back into legitimate land. His friend lumbered after him. His legs were shaking. I walked out more slowly. I had realized the whistle was meant for someone else. But my mouth was a bit dry and I had very little time to eat my own roti and potato curry.

All afternoon, I kept thinking of what Tree Boy had told me about Rafi. Was Rafi up to something? Surely, he couldn't have drunk all his father's beer! Of course not. He was with his parents watching cartoon films, probably sitting between them. But did he have friends who broke into houses and stole things? Was Rafi part of a gang? A criminal gang? My head was so full of these thoughts that when Mrs Guhan suddenly called out my name and demanded to know where the Isle of Wight was, I said, "I can't see any light."

Of course I was punished. I had to stand up and read out aloud a report on the winds around the British Isles. The report was full of Scottish and Welsh names. I stumbled over every one of them. Mrs Guhan, has a special love for the British Isles, and the blasted winds that have nothing better to do than blow about night and day. According to Mrs Guhan, these wind movements add to our general knowledge about climate change. These idiotic winds are not even in our syllabus.

I was now the declared clown of my class and as a great honour, Twinkle escorted me right up to my house that day, giggling all the way. My sister seemed to have already left for home, so I was stuck with Twinkle. Luckily, her four-legged companion was not with her. As we neared home, she said she had something to say to my sister. I was desperate. Then I had a brainwave. I squeezed past her and unlatched the gate. I slid in, and after having latched the gate firmly, I said, "So sorry. I think my father is home for lunch today. I think I can hear his voice."

Twinkle was nervous of my father. She shrugged her shoulders and turned away. The lie did not taste good in my mouth.

When I went in I found that Rafi, the other pain in my life, had come to borrow a book from my mother, a book on psychology. That was curious enough. What he did next, was even more strange. He didn't leave even after he had been given the book. He kept hanging around, my grandparents were at the table, waiting to be served tea and snacks, and yet, the man would not go. My mother finally asked whether he would like something to eat, and he said, "No, no, no" several times.

Then after he had shuffled about some more, and after showing a great interest in our curtains, examining them closely for some time, he left.

The Tree Boy was right. I had to keep an eye on Rafi.

I don't know why my mother and sister did not notice anything strange in his behaviour. I did see them glancing at each other in a meaningful way but I could not understand why.

Something else happened earlier that same day. As I was going up to class after the lunch break, Miss Swami stopped Ma at the second landing. "O Neel," she said with her plastic smile, "I do hope you will contribute to the wall newspaper. You write so well."

She said all this more loudly than she need have and I wondered why, as I murmured, "I'll try, Ma'am" to her. Then as I walked on to class, I saw Mrs D'Souza standing at the door of 10A, two doors away from my classroom. So that was it!

Although I had sort of decided not to submit anything to the wall newspaper, I changed my mind after Miss Swami spoke to me. Why shouldn't I give in a poem? In fact, I didn't even have to write a new one. I already had something which I had written during the winter holidays. I decided to use that.

ABBREVS

Orthopaedicians are called orthos
That's easy to say
But opthalmologists are not opthos
At work or in play.
Pediatricians are not called peds
That doesn't fit the bill
Dentists are not called dents
Dents are what they fill.
Psychiatrists have another name
They are often called shrinks
That's a curious word for a doctor
Who tells us how to think.
If surgeons are called cutters
Since that's what they do
Then, what a psychiatrist does
Must really be true.

Help! I don't want a shrink
To examine my brain
My brain is already so small
That nothing might remain.

On the last day for submitting our entries to the wall newspaper, as the class filed out at lunch break, I stayed behind for a minute and gave my poem to Mrs Guhan. She looked puzzled till I told her what it was. Then she gave me a broad smile and said, "I'm so glad you are submitting something. Nobody else has."

When I went down, I found, to my relief, that Twinkle was already seated with some girls from our class and talking away. As I crossed the group, I heard her say loudly, "Some people are such liars."

This business of talking extra loudly for other people to hear, seems to be in fashion. Did Twinkle want me to hear what she said?

It turned out that I had guessed right.

Since I didn't have to hide from Twinkle, I sat with a couple of my class fellows, who kept on talking about the marks they had got in the maths unit test. Since they had all got much better marks that me, and yet thought they deserved more, I had nothing at all to say to them.

After school, I took my football and went quite bravely to F block. Twinkle was obviously put off with me. I was a free citizen again. Ari was sitting in his usual place, chucking stones in his usual way. He did not notice me even when I went up to him. That was strange. Ari always had a ready smile as if he was really glad to see you. But that day, he ignored me and kept on chucking stones at the tree, till I said, "Hey! What's happened? Bad mood or what?"

Then he looked up and to my utter shock, he snarled, "Do you expect me to smile like a jackass all the time?"

I must have stood there gaping at him for a full minute and a half. Then abruptly, he stood up and gave me a hug, "Sorry. Really sorry," he said. "I have a bit of a headache."

"Let's not play then," I suggested.

But he was already rolling the ball under his feet and I joined him. We raced around the ground, while he showed me how to use the different parts of my foot to direct the ball. "Learn how to curve it," he shouted as he ran. "You should not always pass straight. The idea is to fool your opponent. Fool them."

I was to remember these words for a long time.

As I walked home sweating, I wondered why I liked Ari so much more than my classmates. I did not even know him properly. And there were so many puzzling things about him. Why wasn't he in school or college? He had said something about having to wait to get admission but didn't that mean he would lose a year? What were his parents like? Did he have any brothers and sisters?

I seemed to be surrounded by questions that swarmed around me. About Rafi. About Ari. About Twinkle. About the gang of thieves. As I walked home under a darkening sky,

I saw a woman hurrying the other way. It was Pachamma, her face half covered with some red cloth as if she was cold. She went past me without any sign of recognition. I wondered if I had become invisible.

My father solved the Twinkle mystery over dinner. That loud remark she had made, about some people being liars, had been meant for me. Apparently, Twinkle had seen my father in the market, where he had gone to pick up our dry-cleaned clothes on his way home from office.

"A strange girl," my father said. "Can't remember her name. The Bhonjo girl. She came up to me and asked what I had eaten for lunch on Tuesday. Now, why should she ask me that?"

I heaped food into my mouth.

"Anyway," my father said when nobody answered his question, "I told her I had to skip lunch that day because I was at a meeting that dragged on. For some reason, she seemed rather happy about what I said."

"Maybe she wants you to lose some weight," my uncle guffawed.

"Nonsense," my grandmother snapped. "Your brother is as thin as a curry leaf. He doesn't eat enough."

The conversation drifted into an argument between my grandparents and my uncle on the fatness and thinness of curry leaves. My father finished his food, excused himself and left the table.

As we cleared up, my sister whispered, "So that's why she's going around the whole school, calling you a liar."

I nodded. "She wanted to come in that day," I whispered back. "And I could only think of saying that Dad had come home for lunch. Who thought she would bump into him and..."

My sister gave me a sudden hug. "Never mind what she says," she murmured. "Nobody in school pays any attention to that girl. Actually, I feel sorry for her. But I must tell you, she's not chasing you, she's..."

At that moment, the phone rang and my sister dashed off to answer it. My sister's phone chats take very, very long so instead of waiting to hear what more she had to say about Twinkle, I went up to my room.

As it turned out, I ought to have waited.

It was only the next day that I realized that the phone call was not from any of my sister's friends. It was an urgent call for my father from the Inspector, Mr Khan. There had been another robbery, an attempted one, in E block. The person living there was an old gentleman who had lived abroad, in Nigeria or somewhere, all his life. When he retired, he came back to India and bought this house. He was not married, he lived alone except for a man cook who stayed in the house. A maid used to come and clean twice a day. The old gentleman, Mr Karve, seemed to have no friends, only a nephew who used to visit him once a month. What

happened that afternoon was that the old man suddenly fell very ill. The cook phoned the nephew chap but before he could arrive, the old gentleman became worse so the cook told the maid to rush out and get an auto. They both carried the gentleman into the auto and took him to hospital. When the nephew arrived, he rang the bell, but nobody came to the front door. So he went round to the back of the house. He found the backdoor open, and went in. He found a lot of stuff, valuable stuff, on the floor and a few bags. He was gazing in surprise at all this, when he was hit from behind and he fell unconscious. As soon as he came back to consciousness, he phoned the police. The last thing he remembered as he fell was that there was some shouting, and a lot of running footsteps.

I got to know all this only the next morning. When I came down for breakfast, I found only my sister and my grandparents at the dining table. It was then that my sister gave me the news. "I waited to tell you everything," my sister said. She looked worried. "I knew Mum and Dad would not have the time this morning. Mum is already at a meeting of the Residents' Association."

"Where has Dad gone?" I asked.

"To the hospital," she said. "That old gentleman is better but he has to be told about the attempted burglary. So Dad has gone with the nephew and Mr Khan to break the news gently."

"Did the police find any clues?" I asked, after a pause. I was a detective too I remembered.

"I don't know," my sister replied. "The police are at the house now, examining everything I think. We have to wait to know anything more."

School seemed unusually quiet that day. Even the small kids were less noisy. Teachers stood about in groups outside classroom doors, whispering to each other. This was very, very strange. Usually, they watched us with the eyes of an eagle waiting to pounce on an untied shoelace or a rumpled tie or a chewing jaw. But that day, a lot of trailing shoelaces and untidy ties and steadily moving jaws went past them. It was not just that. News floated around the school that the police were in the Principal's office talking to her and some senior teachers. I don't know why but this news made us all feel guilty. I know I did and I think everyone else in my class did too. There was a lot of smoothing down of hair and straightening of ties. Little wads of paper sticky with gum were quietly chucked into the waste paper basket. Everybody was very, very attentive and asked questions, even in the civics class, about how to fold the national flag in the correct patriotic way. I could see that everyone kept an eye on the door and when somebody sneezed, we all jumped.

When I came home, I found my sister had already reached and my father arrived soon after me. "I want you both to come to the emergency meeting," my father told us. "Your uncle will stay at home till we get back."

My uncle opened his mouth but closed it without a word, when he took a look at my father's face.

The hall was full to bursting. Everyone seemed to be there, both the Doongaji sisters, the entire Bhonjo family without the dog, several school parents, some of my classmates, and many others I did not know. My mother went up to the sisters and sat down next to them. I was surprised to see that Rafi and his parents were absent, as also the Tree Boy. But there was a gentleman who looked exactly as the Tree Boy would look after he grew up, that I was sure he was the father. Then I saw that Ari was there too, alone.

I sat with my sister and my father. Actually, it was the right thing to do because the Inspector looked at my father several times, as if for advice, and I felt that many people noticed this. Afterwards, when I mentioned this to my mother at home, she said I had imagined it. "The Inspector is a senior officer," she said, "and he would be careful not to show any particular friendship towards anybody."

Even so, I was quite sure my mother was wrong. Because why should so many school fellows come and talk to me after the meeting was over? These chaps had never even said hello to me in school.

The meeting began with the Inspector saying that he had posted extra constables in the colony so those who had come to the meeting, need not be afraid that they had left their houses empty. At this point, Twinkle shouted, “It’s alright, Sir, about our house. Our dog is guarding it.” Before she could say anything more, her mother, sitting next to her, shushed her.

The Inspector completely ignored the interruption. He went on with his speech, beginning with the news that senior Mr Karve who had taken ill was back home. “He is suffering from a viral flu,” the Inspector said. “His temperature had shot up and, because of his age, he became delirious. He will be fine within a week, the doctors have told me. He is, of course, very shocked about the attempted burglary in his house. And he asked me the same question that we have been asking each other. Who has been giving them the information that such and such house is suddenly empty? In each case, the residents had left suddenly and unexpectedly. And within minutes, the gang has broken into the house.”

One of the Doongaji sisters raised her arm. “Mr Inspector,” she said, “are you saying somebody is watching us all the time?”

The Inspector paused before he answered. “It seems that way, Ma’am. But in a colony this size and quite spread out, how can such a watch be kept up? Unless…” The Inspector stopped and looked around. “Unless…” he said again.

One of the Banjo brothers spoke. “Unless there is a watcher posted at every block,” he said.

The Inspector looked at him with one of his keen glances. "That's possible," he said. "But how do these watchers send a signal to the rest of the gang?"

There was a murmur of voices in the hall. I heard someone say "smoke signals" and someone else say "nonsense". Then I saw Ari raise his arm. The Inspector smiled and asked, "Yes young man? What do you think?"

"Could it be in some kind of code language?" Ari asked. The Inspector's eyes became more alert.

"What exactly do you mean?" he wanted to know.

Before Ari could answer, one of the Banjo brothers said loudly, "Marking the gate of the empty house?"

The Inspector turned to look at him with another of his sharp looks. "Something like that I suppose," he said.

Then one of the Doongaji sisters spoke up. "But there has to be somebody who does that," she said. "Somebody who may not do the actual theft but gives the thieves information in a clever way."

Nobody spoke for a while. Then the Inspector said, "We are looking at all these angles. Meanwhile, if any of you see anyone acting a little suspiciously, please inform us, the police. Please do not do anything on your own. I have posted additional constables across the colony and also strengthened the night watch. We will do our best to keep you all and your property safe. Thank you."

The meeting broke up after that. The Doongaji sisters came up to talk to my father and I slipped out of their hugs to try and catch Ari. But he had gone.

I remember feeling very agitated after what the Inspector had said about reporting anyone behaving strangely. Should I say anything about Rafi? But except for his staying on at our place and peeping through the curtains, there was nothing I could tell the Inspector. It was the Tree Boy who had seen more of Rafi's strange behaviour, not me. My parents and my sister stayed on in the meeting hall, talking to different people but I decided to go back home. As I walked down the road, the question about Rafi kept troubling me. What was I to do?

I thought of it for a long time, thinking that I should report it to the Inspector and the next moment feeling I shouldn't. And then, in the weird way he had, the Tree Boy crashed into me. This time, instead of falling we clutched each other and wheeled around, like a pair of Sumo wrestlers without the tummies.

The Tree Boy was almost out of breath but he managed to say, "It's all over. They have come to arrest him. I told you, didn't I? I told you then itself. I told you…"

"Hey," I said. "Hold on. What are you talking about? Who is the 'they'? Who is the 'he'?"

The Tree Boy, now in breath, clicked his tongue irritably, as if he was some hundred-year-old teacher of Sanskrit.

"He-e. Your neighbour," he said. "The police are in his house." "What!" I exclaimed. "But the Inspector is still there in the..."

The Tree Boy gave me one of his controlled exasperation looks. I have often seen my grandmother look at my grandfather in the same way.

"Oho," the Tree Boy said in the same grandmother-ish way. "Aren't there other officers in our police force? The...the Sheriff, the ACP, the DSP, the SHO, the FBI..."

"Wait!" I shouted. "How do you know that any of these abbreviations are in his house?"

That look again and then, "Because," he said, slowly drawing out each word, "there is a police jeep outside his house."

That stumped me. "A police jeep?" I asked. "Yes. P-O-L-I..."

"But did you see them arrest him," I asked in a masterful, I hope, way. "Did you see them, with your own eyes, put handcuffs on him?"

"N-no," the Tree Boy admitted. "There was a chap at the gate. Tcha. I should have taken a ball, then I could have thrown it in when he wasn't looking...and..."

But I didn't wait to listen to his stupid plan. I rushed off to check on the police jeep outside Rafi's house. Behind me I heard the Tree Boy's thudding shoes and his voice still babbling. I turned the corner towards our block and looked.

There was no police jeep anywhere in sight.

Instead I saw Mrs Raj and another neighbour, Mrs Zaidi, talking. That is, Mrs Raj was talking and Mrs Zaidi seemed to be in a trap, having to listen. "...So then I sayd I weel put hot mastard oil on you," I heard Mrs Raj say. "Mastard oil is..."

I slowed down. Did she actually say this to the police officer? Had she threatened him with hot mustard oil?

Then Mrs Raj caught sight of me. "Ay!" she called. "Why you not coming to see my poor Rafi? He is very, very seek. Now he is wanting dog also. He is saying some boy spying on heem. You know thees boy? He is from your school only."

I turned to see whether the Tree Boy was still behind me. He had disappeared.

Of course, I disappeared too before either lady could catch me for their own different reasons. Later that day, after dinner, my mother told my sister and me that we should be very careful whom we talk to, especially if it was a stranger. This I thought was weird because my sister and I hardly met any stranger. We went to school and came home, did our homework, I played football and then we had dinner and went off to sleep. We did not even watch television, because that was meant mostly for my grandparents and sometimes my parents. My mother's warning made me think of how my sister and I lived inside a very small globe, which consisted of our school, home and the colony. I must say that when I thought of it this way, I saw myself suddenly as a micro dot inside a decimal point.

I felt quite depressed. Was this part of growing up too?

FEBRUARY

Nothing much happened in the following few days. At school, the new notice board came up with our contributions. My poem had been taken, there were a few cartoons, some more poems and six or seven jokes, two of which I had heard before. There was one poem which I really liked written by a Class 6 student, called "Dear Yelakki Banana". There was no name at the bottom. That was strange. I copied it into my rough book to show my mother. As I was heading home after school, the Tree Boy bumped into me. Again. My school bag helped me from falling flat on my back.

"Hey, great poet," the Tree Boy shouted even as I tried to stop him from calling me that. Then he came close and whispered, "Did you see what I have written?"

"What?" I asked. "I mean where? I mean what? I mean where what? And stop crashing into me," I added. "I think I've got a concussion."

"No, you haven't," he said in a normal voice. "You haven't even hurt your little finger."

I was about to point out that little fingers have nothing to do with concussion when he whispered again, "Did you see my poem on the notice board?" he hissed. "The yelakki banana one?"

I told him I had seen it and read it. "But," I asked. "Why haven't you put your name there? And anyway, why are you bombing my eardrums with your whispers?"

"Because," he hissed on, "the poem has a double meaning. It is a code, can't you see? I told teacher and she said it was alright if I did not put my name."

"What code?" I was quite irritated by this time. "What double meaning?"

He dropped his voice into the underworld. "Fruits become rotten, isn't it?" he said. "So do secrets. That person, you-know-who, has been warned. I am…"

Someone came up from behind me, coughing badly. The Tree Boy stopped his snake hiss abruptly. The next second, he was gone.

I turned and saw Rafi, bent double with coughing. There was a gaggle of his classmates, all female, hovering around him, one holding out a bottle of water, another some cough drops, the third a paper tissue. All their faces had the expression that hospital nurses have.

Some men are so lucky, I thought. Then I noticed Twinkle running up and I followed the example of the Tree Boy. I fled.

It was Pachamma who gave us the next bit of news. "Police are asking boys and girls why you not go to school? That is what they are asking."

We were in the dining hall, just finishing tea, I remember. My father and uncle were not at home, my grandfather was in the drawing room, reading, but the rest of us were around. My sister had brought out the scrabble board and we were vaguely arranging words on it. When Pachamma made her dramatic announcement, my grandmother dismissed it saying, "Must be the Government programme, compulsory education for all children."

"No, Amma, no," said Pachamma in her shrillest voice. "This is not govenament thing OK. This is about thieves and all."

We waited. My sister stopped fiddling with the letter tiles. Pachamma took position like the coach of a football team before a big match. "I told Amma I not come today morning because police stopped me in F block itself," she said. "They asked me so many many questions. Who who boy, girl did not went to school that day. You know that day? That poor man he go to hospital? That day only."

I was puzzled. Why should the police want to know who was absent from school that day? Then I saw my sister's face, white and pinched looking, and suddenly I understood.

"So what did you say?" my mother asked, her voice very troubled.

"What I could say?" Pachamma said. "What I know? I go, do work and go, that is all."

I felt my sister relax. But Pachamma had not finished. She went on. "What I know about children? Only that third boy in that big house where they have big big music was at home only that day. When I put clothes outside, he was in upstairs I saw. And also the next door boy, you know. He also in house only."

"He has high fever," my sister said in a defiant kind of way. Pachamma sniffed and shrugged her shoulders. My sister was about to say something more when my mother spoke.

"There can be many reasons why children miss school," she said. "Genuine reasons. Finish your work, Pachamma. Everything has got late today."

My mother and Pachamma left the room. My grandmother went out too, murmuring, for some reason, "Everything has got late today, everything has got higgledy-piggledy."

My sister looked at me and asked in a very hesitant way, "Neel, do you think that..."

"I think," I said firmly, "that you should stay away from Rafi. He has a really bad viral fever."

And then we hugged each other, my sister and I and she rested her face against my arm for a moment. Later, I found my T-shirt sleeve was wet.

After dinner, when everyone was in the drawing room, looking rather depressed, I decided to read out the Tree Boy's poem. It was called "Dear Yelakki Banana".

Dear yelakki banana,

  Why do you change colour so soon?

  You were bright yellow this morning

but have got so dark by noon.
I know yelakki is cardamom
Whose colour is a green brown
But why do you turn black
Just to show you've grown?
O! Now I am in a fix!
Brown does not rhyme with grown,
English spellings and yelakki bananas
Do make a poet groan.

The poem was a great success. My grandfather clapped, my grandmother said she had never liked yelakki bananas, my parents said it was a clever bit of verse, and my sister smiled. My uncle, loudly and repeatedly declared that this young man was a genius and would, one day, out-Tagore Tagore. After this declaration, there was a fierce argument between my grandparents and my uncle about how anyone could out-Tagore Tagore. My grandfather said that the phrase out-Tagoring Tagore was nonsensical. My uncle said he had only used the term out-Tagore, Tagore, not out-Tagoring Tagore. My grandfather said it came to the same thing, and that was how any army commander would see it. My grandmother said several times that Tagore had written our national anthem and also the national anthem for Bangladesh and he was great friends with Gandhi. While the battle raged on, the rest of us slipped out, first my father, then my mother and my sister, then I.

I don't know when truce was declared, if ever it was. Because next morning, something greatly unexpected happened. My uncle announced that the police had made an arrest.

We knew about this only the next morning as we were eating breakfast. My uncle, whose meal times always seemed to be according to countries south of the equator, rushed in with wild eyes and rumpled hair.

"Guess what!" he yelled. "Just guess what…"

Before anyone of us could open our tongues, he shouted, "They have got the wrong man. I am telling you he is not the man. Just because he is poor and works hard for a living, they have done this. I am going to write about this. The police are tyrants…I tell…"

My father excused himself and got up to put on his shoes. When my uncle went on about the callousness of the police system and its insensitivity, my father looked up and said, "Nobody has been arrested. Please do not spread rumours. The police are looking for Mani, who seems to have seen something. It may or may not be important. In the meanwhile, I suggest you restrain the kindness of your nature."

My uncle stomped off. My sister and I finished breakfast and left for school. I was wondering who Mani was, when my sister said, "He is the man who comes once in three or four months from Tamil Nadu to bring down coconuts from our tree. You should see how he goes up the tree. He is quite amazing."

We have two very tall coconut trees in our front garden. How was it that I had never seen this man Mani? Not seen his athletic skills? Was I so unobservant? I felt ashamed of myself. What kind of detective was I?

It was a bland day at school. Classes went on as usual, there were quizzes, questions not answered properly or completely and there were the absentees, which included Twinkle. This of course, was a blessing. I sat with some boring class fellows who talked endlessly about what entrance exams they were aiming to do after Class 12, and how much their first pay packet would be. I wished the Tree Boy would bump into me, but he was nowhere to be seen.

By the time I got back home after school, I had forgotten all about Mani. That's what routine does, it sort of deadens you.

But when I reached home, there was excitement pouring out of the windows. No, it was not Pachamma holding centre stage but a little white blob of woolliness, whose name, I was told, was Dog. Rafi's of course. It was sitting on his lap, looking very important and jumping a bit every time Rafi coughed. My family, except for my father and my uncle, was gathered around the little blob, exclaiming at its smallness, its sharpness and its impressive name. As far as my family is concerned, anything that Rafi does, is to be admired and praised to the skies. So I was about to cross the drawing room and go off, when suddenly, the little blob jumped off its master's lap, came toddling up to me and began licking my shoes.

Dog became my best friend. Rafi did not like that at first and I think he tried to keep him away from me. But Dog had a mind of his own and Rafi had to give up at the end. Now of course, things are quite different. Anyway, Dog had massive dislikes too. He couldn't stand Pachamma and bared his teeth at her, rather like a vampire. She was equally hostile to him. Once when she thought nobody was around, she aimed a kick at him. She missed, naturally, and she also got a thorough scolding from my mother who had seen the futile kick.

Everybody else in our house adored Dog as much as they adored his master. This part I did not like very much but there was nothing I could do about it.

In the meanwhile, all the maids and the gardeners and the vegetable sellers who went around the colony with push carts, were looking for the coconut tree climber, Mani. The trouble was that nobody seemed to know what he looked like. This is, of course, very useful for crooks; to look so ordinary, that nobody could describe them. But there was a bigger problem with Mani. When owners of coconut trees were asked who brought down the coconuts for them, they mentioned other names. Somebody said it was a man called Appan, another said he was Senthil, a third called him Mowgli. But they all said the man came from Tamil Nadu.

My uncle who brought us all this information in bits and pieces, began shouting at us, as usual. "This is the problem with us. We are elitists. We don't know what Mani looks like. Why? Because we don't look at him. We don't know whether he is short or tall, or bald or… If it was somebody of our class, would we have been so blind? Tell me. Would we have been so blind?"

None of us answered. We were sitting in the drawing room after dinner, my father had not yet come home. My mother was knitting, my grandfather was leafing through some book, my grandmother was examining her fingers, my sister looked as if she was half asleep and I was thinking of Ari and football tactics. Then my uncle said something that made me switch my thoughts to him.

"I'm going to get to the bottom of this," he declared grandly. "The police are no good. I am going to trace this man or men from Tamil Nadu. I will find him or them. I will."

I was very impressed by these words. I am not often impressed by my uncle but this time, I realized that he was going to do some detective work. And I had given up detection. So, once he had stopped his speechifying, I asked my uncle, "May I come with you if it is after school?"

He considered my request as if he was a judge at an elocution contest. "Alright," he said finally, "but you must follow my instructions to the T".

I was about to ask what this "T" was, but just then, my mother, with a note of alarm in her voice, said, "Please don't get Neel into any kind of trouble."

My uncle snorted. "Ha!" he said, "it will help him grow up."

My mother still looked worried and I gave her a hug. "I will be fine Mum," I whispered. "I will try and keep him out of trouble."

She laughed then.

My uncle's methods of detection baffled me. The first time I went out with him, all he did was walk around the colony, with his hands in his pockets and whistling something totally tuneless. Before we started on "our truth campaign" as he called it, my uncle gave some instructions. I was supposed to walk a few paces behind him, and to "note down anything suspicious".

"Like what?" I asked.

"How do I know like what?" he rasped. "That's your job. And while we are at this job, don't speak to me or even exchange glances with me. Nobody should know we are connected."

"But," I protested. "Most people know you are my uncle."

He ignored this. My uncle, like a lot of adults, is very good at ignoring what he doesn't want to hear.

So we set out late that afternoon, my uncle sauntering in front, as if he was a tourist, and I, a few metres behind him, feeling like a fool.

We walked around the roundabout in the middle of our colony, with its sullen, green pool and the dead fountain. My uncle raised a hand in greeting to Sundar, the ironing man whose work-cart is at one end of the road. Earlier, Sundar used to come to each house and take the clothes himself and return them, ironed, in the evening. Now he is so busy that the maids have to take the clothes to him, and bring them back once they are done. I know all about this, because sometimes, I have had to do the clothes carrying.

Anyway, my uncle, who usually chats with everyone he meets, did not stop to talk to Sundar. Maybe this was because he was being a "detective" or because Sundar is a bit of a surly fellow. I saw a couple of maids hurry up to Sundar's cart with bundles of clothes which he and his equally surly assistant unwrapped. Then rapidly, they began counting the number of garments. I find it quite amazing how they know which clothes belong to which bundle and to which house. As far as I know, Sundar hardly ever makes a mistake. I remember my mother telling me once, that a book on workers like Sundar would be very interesting to read. She said that those who studied sociology would find it a good project. Hm.

Well, my uncle and I walked on, going around each block. Now and then, my uncle would stop outside a house where there was one or perhaps two coconut trees and stare up. What did he expect to see up a tree on a darkening winter evening? Then he would rub his nose as if he was "detecting" very hard and walk on. Finally, we limped home, without finding a single coconut tree climber.

I was pretty disappointed but my uncle insisted on saying, as we were walking homewards, that we had done a good "recce".

"Did you note down the number of coconut trees in the colony?" he asked me. I said I hadn't.

"But I told you to!" he shouted, stopping at the gate of our house.

"You told me to note down anything suspicious," I shouted back. "What is so suspicious about a coconut tree?"

My uncle started shouting again. My mother came out and made us stop. Then she asked me to apologize to my uncle. I kept saying that he had shouted first and had said something unfair, but I had to say "sorry" to him.

Of course I did not like to do this and I almost thought of going to sleep without eating dinner, just to show them. But I was terribly hungry.

I felt a little cheered at dinner, because my grandfather called my uncle a fool for thinking that coconut tree climbers from Tamil Nadu, would be found in Bengaluru in the months of January and February.

"They all go back home for the harvesting season," he said and went back to his food. My uncle stayed quiet as did the rest of us.

It was my sister who broke the silence. "My friends in school told me something quite strange," she said. "Apparently, the police are looking for Mani because a message was pushed through a window of the police station by someone. It was a piece of paper torn from a notebook and it was in some kind of code."

"Code?" I asked.

"Yes," replied my sister. "There was a picture of what seemed to be a coconut tree, then the picture of a pair of eyes and then the name Mani, in capital letters."

I swallowed my food quickly and went upstairs as soon as I could to think. Code! Who had talked so much about codes?

The Tree Boy! Had he written that message to the police? I had to catch him. I had to know.

I went to school a little early the next day, along with my sister who is usually there before me. I loitered near the gate to catch the Tree Boy but though I stood there till the bell rang, I did not see him. I could not catch sight of him at morning break either, nor at lunch. This was strange. Of course, he may have fallen ill or broken a leg or something. But how was I to find out? I did not know any of his class fellows. I did not even know which class he was in. Then I suddenly remembered his friend, the nervous fellow, the one who jumped every time PT Ma'am blew her whistle. Would I be able to find him?

I stood near the gate again after school, looking for the Tree Boy's friend, the nervous chap. I wasn't very sure whether I would recognize him even if I saw him. All boys of the same size, wearing the school uniform, crumpled and a little dirty at the end of the day, look the same. I waited by the gate till the school had almost emptied itself out. But I couldn't see anyone looking like Jumper. Then, I heard PT Ma'am's whistle, loud, impatient, and in the direction of a gaggle of uniforms lingering near the gate, and I saw a small figure jump ten feet high. Well, almost.

I had got my man, the Jumper.

He jumped again, but not as much, when I slapped my hand on his shoulder. He tried to scuttle off but I caught his arm firmly, and asked, "Where is ..."

That is when I remembered that I didn't know the Tree Boy's actual name. This is what comes of giving nicknames, I thought to myself.

But I still kept hold of Jumper, another nickname. He was pulling away so hard that he had dragged me outside the school gate by now. He calmed down then and asked, "Where's who?"

"Your friend," I said. "Your best friend." I hoped to goodness I was right about that.

Jumper seemed to understand whom I meant. Perhaps he had only one friend, best or not.

"Absent for four days," Jumper said. "He has gone to Tamil Nadu."

"What?" I was so startled that I let go of his arm. He shot away and I was forced to shout out my next question. "What for?" I asked wondering whether the Tree Boy too, had gone for the harvesting season.

"For a wedding," Jumper shouted back from far down the road.

The Tree Boy had been absent for four days. So he couldn't have sent that coded message. Who could that have been? And most important, how were we to find the mysterious man from Tamil Nadu, Mani, the coconut tree climber?

Help came from an unexpected quarter. Milind Karve, the nephew of the old gentleman who had been taken ill, came to meet my father, to thank him for all his help. This Mr Karve had also been admitted to hospital because he had been hit at the back of his head and fallen unconscious. He came on a Saturday afternoon, when we were all at home, my uncle too. Junior Mr Karve still had a strip of bandage at the back of his head.

"Luckily, it was not a serious blow," he said. "But the doctors had to cut away some of my hair in that area, so I am sure my head looks very funny from behind."

"You only look like a brave soldier," my grandfather boomed and my grandmother twittered, "If you wear a cap, nobody will notice."

My father asked how his uncle, senior Mr Karve was doing.

"He is very well," was the reply. "He has recovered quite remarkably. Today, he was out in the garden, scolding the man who gets down the coconuts from the only tree there is. He was…"

My uncle interrupted him with his usual shout, "Is the man's name Mani?" Mr Karve was a bit startled at the fierceness of the question.

"I'm not very sure," he said. "I think I heard my uncle call by some other name."

"Can you find out?" my uncle asked, lowering his voice a little. And as an afterthought, he added, "please".

My father cleared his throat and explained to our visitor that the police were trying to trace a man called Mani.

"So far, they haven't been able to," said my father.

"That is because," my grandfather butted in, "all these chaps from Tamil Nadu go off for the harvesting season."

"Ah!" Mr Karve responded. "So this man, whom the police are looking for, is from Tamil Nadu, is it?"

We all nodded vigorously.

"That's interesting," Mr Karve said, smiling. "My uncle was speaking to this man in Tamil this morning. In rather poor Tamil, I must say, a sort of mixture of Tamil and Hindi."

My father deftly turned the conversation away from the police investigation at this point, and began talking about how we Indians speak so many different languages, and without thinking too much about it.

My uncle glared at my father but that was of no use because Mr Karve had already started talking about his attempts at learning Kannada. He spoke with a lot of humour and soon we were all laughing at how he got the words mixed up and said something when he meant something else. Only my uncle refused to laugh and would not take part in the conversation. I thought he was behaving very childishly. Here was our visitor from a different part of India, sitting comfortably with a family he had just met, and laughing at himself for the mistakes he made while learning an unknown language. I thought then of the rich collection of languages we had in our country. And of all the stories there were in each language. How strange that our conversation was mostly in English but did that matter? This "foreign" language was bringing us together.

As Mr Karve was leaving, after thanking my parents again and taking leave of the rest of us, he turned to my uncle and said, "I will ask my uncle to send this man to meet you. I overheard them saying he would be doing some gardening for my uncle tomorrow morning."

My uncle got his smile back. Then he said something that I liked very much. My uncle said, "Mr Karve, this colony is really a mini-India. The residents here come from different parts of the country, speak different languages, worship different gods, eat different foods. Yet we are all part of the human family. These differences are not, in any way, divisions."

My grandmother wiped her eyes, and said softly, "That is how all our great leaders like Gandhi, wanted India to be."

My grandfather spoke louder and more gruffly, "Our only religion is the great Constitution of India. It is a remarkable document and we must all live by it."

Mr Karve bowed to my grandparents and left.

It was only much later, as I went up to my room that I realized that my grandmother had used the past tense when she spoke of India.

Had she seen something of what was to happen and which shattered us all?

Early next morning, which was a Sunday, we were eating breakfast—my uncle was still asleep—when we heard a lot of shouting at the gate. My father went out to see what was happening and came back after some time, with a curious tale.

"That was our gardener," he said, "arguing with the missing coconut tree climber, Mani."

"Mani!" I yelled. "We've found him! Wow!" I was about to rush out when my father stopped me. "You are getting more like your uncle every day," he said, but with a smile. "Listen to the rest of the story first. It seems Mani is not our man's name at all."

"But we have always called him Mani," my mother said.

"Well, our gardener Chinna Thambi says he is Senthil," my father said. "Is it the same person?"

"Yes, it is," my mother replied. "I saw him through the window. Just let me clear the table and I will come out and talk to him."

In the end, my sister and I helped clear the table and then rushed out. My grandparents were already out in the garden, examining a small man with darting eyes who kept his hands in a permanent state of prayer. Our gardener, Chinna Thambi was standing near him, in a military stance, as if to protect all our bushes and grasses and plants from this man.

My mother spoke to the small man in Tamil, asking him his name. "Are you Mani?" she asked.

He nodded.

"He told me he is Senthil," Chinna Thambi shouted. "I have not seen him in this house but when I see him anywhere in the colony, he says he is Senthil."

We all looked at Mani Senthil to see what he had to say. He said nothing, He only smiled and bowed.

"Do you have two names?" my father asked him quietly. He beamed and nodded.

"Do you have any more names, Mani?" my mother asked, also very quietly.

At this point, there was a thundering sound inside the house, of someone knocking down several pieces of furniture, then using several curse words. My uncle emerged as if from a typhoon.

"What is all this infernal noise," he snarled, "on a Sunday morning?" Then he noticed Mani Senthil and greeted him in surprise. "Ay Mowgliappa!" my uncle said. "You here? I have been looking all over for you da. Do you know a man called Mani?"

Finally, after all the arguing and the shouting between my uncle and Chinna Thambi, and my grandmother very loudly insisting that he was Mani when he was a boy and always will be Mani, we managed a few minutes of silence. In that oasis, my father asked, "What is your real name please?"

The man with the many names spoke at last. He grinned at all of us, and said, "In one house, when I climb the tree, they call me Mani, in another house when I cut the grass, they call me Mowgliappa, in one another house, where I wash the car, they call me Senthil. Then, in another one house," he added, "they call me Appan."

There was a moment's silence, then my grandfather asked, "You have no problem with all these different names?"

The small man laughed. "No!" he said. "Why to have problem? All good names only."

My grandmother chuckled. "So higgledy-piggledy," she said.

My father and my uncle marched Mani, alias Senthil, alias Mowgliappa, alias Appan, to the police station. When they came back more than an hour later without Mani they said that the police had let the coconut tree climber off. All that Mani seemed to know was that from the perch of a tree, he had seen some tall boy running away from the backdoor of one of the houses. He could neither remember which day it was, nor had he seen the boy's face from far up the tree.

That afternoon, my football practice session with Ari was really exhausting. He made me run up and down the grounds with the ball and then he appeared unexpectedly from somewhere and got the ball away from me. I could not tell where he would come from and so of course, I lost the ball. After half an hour of these "attacks" I was quite sure I would make a lousy forward.

I sat against the railings feeling depressed. Ari did not try to cheer me up in the usual way people do. Instead he asked, "So what happened at home this morning?" This was the first time he had asked me about my life at home. I told him about Mani and his different names and he listened without comment. When I finished he burst out laughing; he laughed quite a lot.

"You tell a story well," he said after he stopped laughing. "You should be a writer."

That cheered me up although it was not about my football skills.

"Your story," Ari went on, "made me realize how little our names matter. Think of it. God is called by so many different names and he never seems to mind."

This statement was so unexpected and difficult to understand that I could only stare at him.

"Anyway," Ari said, half laughing again, "This Mani is quite a character. I hope the police get a lot of information from him. I'm glad I sent that message to them. See you. Bye."

And as quick as a fish, he did what he had never done before. He disappeared, leaving me sitting there as if I was a goalie who had let the net open to a dozen goals.

It was a long time before I could sleep that night. So it was Ari who had written that pictogram message to the police? Why had he not just gone and told them directly? Now, did Ari expect me to tell them? Or had he told me his secret in confidence? Would I be a sneak if I spoke about it? What was I to do?

Finally, I decided that I would go downstairs and talk to my mother. She would most probably be alone and that would make it easier for me. But as I went down the stairs, I heard my father talking. My heart sank. I was never sure of my father. I wondered whether to turn back. But then something he said, stopped me from turning.

"I think both the children have been handling this very well," my father was saying. "Especially Neel. I find him more and more mature these days. He knows when not to speak and when it is essential that he does."

I clambered down the rest of the stairs very noisily and entered the drawing room where my parents were sitting. There was nobody else there and so I was able to unburden myself without swallowing my words.

My parents listened to me in silence, then my father said, "Glad you told us this, son. You must have been very troubled about whether to or not. But put your mind at rest. Your friend went to the police station earlier, and confessed. He had overheard some fellows at the marketplace talking of Mani the coconut man who had seen something. Apparently, he himself felt later that it had been a very childish thing that he had done."

I was very relieved to hear this. Phew. As my parents wished me goodnight, my father gave me a sudden, rare hug. I went back to my room and slept off immediately.

The next day, the school was abuzz with all kinds of rumours. One knot of fellows said that the entire Banjo family had been arrested by the police. Another said "no, only one of them, probably Sirius". A third said, "Hope it was the dog." It was then that I remembered that Twinkle had been absent for two or three days. I had not thought much about it, just felt relieved. But then I also realized that I had not been seeing any of her brothers either. What had they all done?

I saw my sister with her group of friends. Unlike most of the girls around her, she was looking pale and anxious, not gleeful.

I have always wondered why we all feel a little gleeful when other people get into some kind of trouble. Is it because we are comfortable, safe and so we feel superior?

The bell rang. PT Ma'am blew her whistle and the chattering stopped. Assembly began.

It was after the school prayer and the news of the day, that our Principal took the mike. She looked very serious.

"Children, I need to say something very important to you. Please listen carefully. As some of you know, the police have been looking into the thefts that have happened in this colony. In the course of their investigation, they have been questioning a number of people, including some of our senior students. Please note that the police are only asking them questions. Nobody, I repeat, nobody has been arrested. Anybody spreading false rumours will be severely punished. Just attend to your school work and your games and leave police work to the police. Thank you."

We were all very quiet as we filed into our classrooms. I felt very conscious of Twinkle's absence and strangely, I felt a bit sad too. I wondered whether I would allow her to talk to me or walk with me, when she came back. If she did come back.

School was more boring than usual, even the teachers' scolds lacked pulp, they were like squashed lemons. In the last period, which was Hindi, Miss Rupa made a surprise announcement. Miss Rupa usually speaks only in very elevated Hindi which I usually cannot understand. This time however, after all the krupaya and drsyakon, she actually translated it into a language I could understand. Apparently, it was time for us to contribute to OUR noticeboard with OUR thoughts on OUR India. This was the theme given this time. It was so much like an exam question, that I felt sure it was Miss Swami's idea.

"Do you love your country? If so, why? If not, why not?"

"You should submit your entries in a week," said Miss Rupa, and as she finished, Miss Swami poked her face and her painted smile, into the classroom.

"I hope you understood the announcement, children," she chirped, "and will contribute a lot. Your entry could be in the form of a small paragraph, just a couple of lines, a drawing, anything at all. Or a poem perhaps, Neel?"

She giggled and her face with that plastic smile disappeared. The bell rang and we all started to pack our bags and leave in as orderly a way as possible.

Outside, the air was cold and I walked home alone as usual. I wished Ari was in our school, I was sure I would have been able to talk to him about the puzzlements in my mind. Why, for instance, did I dislike Hindi so much? Was it because I had never read a fun book in Hindi? Was it also because almost all my Hindi teachers had been unsmiling people who had taught me the language as if it was a kind of punishment. "Learn this or else!"

How does one love a language? How does one love a country?

How does one love another person, someone who is not part of your family? When will my moustache grow?

I didn't think any of my classmates would be asking themselves these questions. Except maybe, the last one about the moustache. Would Ari have asked himself those other questions?

I was almost home and so deep in my thoughts, that I did not notice a little white bundle waddling towards me. It jumped up to lick me with a very wet tongue. "Can't understand why this fellow loves you so much," said a surly voice from behind me. Rafi. He shifted his heavy school bag and took Dog into his arms and away from me. Dog licked his face madly. Rafi's face. A face with a thin line above the lips. I went home.

We were now well into February and the teachers had gone into revision mode. This meant so many, many tests and so many assignments that I had no time to even think of football. Also, something else happened that was quite nasty. I had gone on a Sunday afternoon to practice with Ari. Unusually, he was not alone. There were some other boys with him. Ari greeted me rather strangely.

"I did not expect you now," he said in a bad-tempered sort of way. "I am trying to get these fellows to play as a team. It's b...y hard. And now you have landed up."

I was taken aback. Ari and I had never fixed any time for our practice and the fellows around him I had never seen before. One of them punched me in the stomach and asked in a jeer, "You write love song? For that dog girl?"

The others laughed.

I mumbled something and walked away. Ari did not stop me.

After this incident, I decided I would not practice football with Ari anymore. I had my terrace and my flower pots, I did not need him. What happened that Sunday afternoon was a shock. I did not tell anyone about it though. I couldn't.

I decided on one more thing. I would focus on my studies and write about the history of India from my point of view, as an ordinary citizen. Our history books talk a lot about what great leaders did and said. But what about ordinary people? They think about their country too. Sometimes. They think about their government, about jobs, about their income, about what they own and what they wish to have. I wanted to write about these things. In ordinary language.

I decided to start off by writing, not a poem, but a small paragraph for the notice board. But how was I to begin? I didn't have even a fraction of an idea.

But things work out in a very curious way sometimes. At dinner that day, my father who is usually very silent, started talking about how some powerful people were wanting to take away a large part of Cubbon Park to build a huge structure for their own use.

"Cubbon Park is a green area we should not touch," my father said. I had not seen him this angry for a long time. "We need parks and woodland to breathe. For children to play. For our birds and butterflies. These people only think of themselves. They are destroying our land, our rivers, our future."

Then my father turned to my sister and me and said, softly, gently, "Neel, Rhea, our generation has done much wrong to this country. But you young people have the power to stop the wrong. You are strong. You can transform our city, our country, our world into a place of peace and happiness. You can. You must."

We were all quiet, even my uncle. My sister ran up and hugged my father. I did too. I noticed that my father had not touched his food.

And so, I began my piece for the school notice board. I found it very difficult. Finally, after many scratched out lines and many torn up sheets, this is what I wrote.

"I do not know whether I love my country or not. When I think of all the poor people of India, of how they live without clean water, without food, without houses, when I see our leaders thinking only of becoming rich and powerful, fighting over language and religion, then I feel our country is the worst in the world. But then I look at my grandmother's face, full of lines and wrinkles and black smudges. It is not beautiful, but there is history in her face, and I am part of that history. I am part of India's history. I have the power to make my country smile again. When my grandmother smiles, her tired eyes light up and she is beautiful once more. My country asks me to make her beautiful again. I love my country."

I wrote out the piece in my best handwriting to show my father before I took it to school. But when I went downstairs, I found everybody in a tizzy. My father had already left the house. My mother was shuttling between the kitchen and the front door and the phone. There had been another robbery.

This time it was in G block. My sister told me about it as we walked to school. "It has the same pattern as all the earlier ones," my sister said. "The old couple had moved to this colony only a fortnight ago. It seems they keep to themselves and never go out together. But they had gone to the bank to open a new account and transfer their money from Delhi."

"Anyway," she said, "even for that little while, they did all the things that people do, to show there was someone in the house. They went out through the back door, they left their washing on the line and they asked the gardener whom they had just hired, to be around in the garden, till they returned. He agreed. But he was of no use."

"The gardener?" I exclaimed. "Our man with the many names?"

My sister did not know. Anyway, what happened was that the gardener, whoever he was, found a warm spot under a tree in the front lawn and went off to sleep. The burglars went into the house by unpicking the lock in the back door and took whatever was valuable, including all the cash.

"When did this happen?" I asked.

"Just yesterday," my sister replied. "Yesterday morning. When the old couple came back, they found the house in a mess and lots of things missing. The gardener was still asleep on the front lawn. He had heard nothing."

"So he says," I murmured.

We had reached the school gates by this time. My sister was swallowed up by her highly excited group of friends and I was accosted by the Tree Boy.

"Back are you?" I was asking, when he pulled me by my bag strap onto the side of the road away from the gates. He was hissing as usual.

"Secret conspiracies in school," he hissed, and all the "s"s sounded sinister. "Look out for the tall guy with spectacles."

"What tall guy with spectacles?" I asked, irritated. "There are millions of tall guys with…"

I heard PT Ma'am's whistle. I saw the Jumper, just about to get into school, jump. The Tree Boy saw him too. But before he scooted, he pulled my ear closer to his hiss and whispered, "Sports..." Then he was off.

I went into school with my head in a whirl. What did he mean "sports"? Did he mean games or someone associated with sports like the Sports Captain? Or the Vice-Captain? Or the Sports Prefect of each house? Was any one of them tall and wearing glasses? And why were we to take note of them? Secret conspiracies? What rubbish. I decided to ignore the Tree Boy's fanciful ideas.

How wrong I was!

At school, everything seemed to be back to normal. Twinkle and her brothers were back, but all of them looked quite subdued. Just before the lunch break, Twinkle was told to go to the Principal's office, and apparently, so were her brothers. They were there for a long time. The buzz was that the Banjo parents had also been called.

One of my class fellows said, rather spitefully, "They are going to close that wretched club of theirs. It seems the police found drugs being passed around there. Music, my foot! I hope it is closed good and proper."

But someone else was sure that would not happen. "I don't think the club will be closed. It should not be. That family is really talented," was his comment.

And a third fellow said, more soberly than the first chap, "I suppose the parents will now check who attends the Saturday club evenings. In any case, I was told that Sirius has a problem with his eyes. So he gets bad marks and does not want to come to school. Nothing to do with drugs."

Whatever it was, I felt relieved. I would not be accosted by a Banjo boy for some time at least. I was not sure of Twinkle though. Not then.

I gave in my piece for the notice board, the students' wall paper, to Mrs D'Souza. She was really pleased that I had written something.

"You know, Neel," she said, in a very un-teacher way, "I am so glad you are continuing to write about these important things. I find that most students only think of marks and what entrance exams they are going to sit for. Many of them only want to know how they can get admission into a foreign university. They hardly think of what is happening around them. You are different."

I was so embarrassed I didn't know what to say.

She spoke again, after a pause. "I suppose much of the praise must be for your parents. They have made you see that there are aspects to life that are as important as getting a good job, being successful at work. But you are all going to be voters in a very few years. How would you like your country to be? Should it not be a place of peace, where everyone lives together without fear, where all views are heard and respected? Your sister is so much like you. She too is concerned about what the country means to her."

My sister? As Mrs D'Souza gave me a pat on the shoulder and walked away, I realized that I had never included my sister in my thoughts about the country. Why didn't I?

I think we all take our families too much for granted. We give much more importance to other people.

I felt ashamed of myself. I decided that from now on, I would talk to my sister the way I talk to myself with all the questions and confusions that my mind holds. However, this did not happen that evening. My sister and my mother were not at home when I got in. My uncle told me that they had gone to visit the old couple who had been robbed.

"Your milk is in a flask on the table," my uncle said. "And there is some nice fruit cake that Mrs Raj sent across."

"Very delicious," my grandmother whispered, without taking her eyes off the television screen. "You will like it."

The television was showing scenes of people protesting in the streets. I could not make out where it was. I went in to have the cake and the milk. The cake was really delicious. Afterwards, I went up to the terrace with my football. I was wondering why my uncle, a journalist, used a silly word like "nice" for the cake, while my grandmother had said "delicious". I remembered that Miss Swami hated the word, "nice" and had once said that it was as useless as a squished tube of toothpaste. But thoughts of Miss Swami and my disillusionment with her were forgotten, as I reached the terrace. The first thing I heard was an enormous volley of barks. For a creature so small, Dog has a very, very loud voice, especially when he sees someone he does not like. Who was it this time? Not Pachamma surely, she was safely in the kitchen. I peered carefully over the terrace wall, keeping my head down as much as possible. An astonishing sight met my eyes. Down below on the road, very near our gates were Twinkle and her four-legged companion. Next door, trying vainly to get through the closed gates, was a furious Dog, barking madly and now and then, letting out a ferocious growl. But that was not the astonishing sight. What was really amazing and unbelievable, was my enemy, that bully dog Tiny, cowering behind Twinkle, whimpering, desperately wanting to get away, pulling at the leash which had wound itself around Twinkle's legs. She was trying to disentangle herself and yelling at the dog at the same time. "Oh, Tiny, don't be a fool," she was screaming. "He is much smaller than you. Look at him. Stand up to him. Be a man. Shut up. Stop crying for heaven's sake. Be a man, man!"

This last command seemed to me, to be quite absurd. I think her pet thought so too because it only whimpered more loudly, shamefully, while Dog continued his enraged, thundering protest.

I have heard from many people, mostly from teachers, that bullies are actually cowards. Now I saw it for myself and it was not at all a pleasant sight. Never did I think I would see that huge fellow who always bared his teeth at me, look so pathetic.

Through the corner of my eye, I saw Rafi standing at the door of his house, laughing not too loudly and clapping, also not too loudly. I too kept myself hidden as much as I could. I did not want to have to shelter either girl or her bully dog. But at least I knew now that I had a fierce little protector almost as good as a Commando. This made me really happy. As I continued to watch the drama down below, I saw Twinkle finally free herself from the leash and get pulled away by her cowardly dog. Rafi came out of hiding and picked up Dog and hugged him. He opened the gate of his house to watch the disappearing duo. I emerged from my kneeling place, and was about to call out to Dog when I saw another astounding sight. I saw my mother and sister turn the corner towards our house but they were not alone. With them, talking very animatedly, was a tall figure. Somebody I knew well but whom I had never seen or expected to see in this part of the colony. It was Ari! As I watched them walking down the road, I saw that Rafi had noticed them too. He stood still with Dog in his arms. And then astonishingly, Dog wriggled himself free, jumped down and bounded up to Ari, his tail wagging as if it was motorized. Ari picked him up with a laugh and Dog, almost panting with adoration, licked him and went on licking his face and neck.

I replay that scene in my mind, even now, my mother and sister, standing there watching Dog, Ari laughing with delight and Rafi stock still, stiff. It was a scene that should have made me aware of a lot of things but it didn't, not then anyway. Abruptly, the scene broke. Rafi called out to Dog, not with much affection. Dog gave Ari a final, wet lick and ran back to his master. Ari laughed louder, and spoke so that his words would carry, "Ah! Possession is nine-tenths of the law!" Then, still laughing, he bowed to my mother and sister and walked away rapidly. All this happened more quickly than my description of it, so quickly that I didn't have the time to gather my wits and dash downstairs and meet Ari, to invite him home.

But he wouldn't come, my mother told me when I went downstairs. "I asked him, but he shook his head. Such a charming boy," she went on, "so polite. He asked me to apologize to you for not playing with you last Sunday. But that you must be there this Sunday. You should go, Neel. He is a fine boy and, I am sure, will be a good friend for you. I know you don't have many friends in school. Did you see how Dog behaved?"

I told her I had seen everything from the terrace. "Well, I don't suppose Rafi liked that much," my mother said and laughed. My sister didn't laugh. Instead, she turned and without saying anything, went up to her room.

Over dinner, my mother talked about her visit to the couple whose house was the latest to have been burgled.

"The old couple, Mr and Mrs Anand, were very polite," my mother said. "But I felt they didn't want us there. As if they wanted to be left alone. You felt that too, didn't you, Rhea?"

My sister nodded. "They were both very sad people," she said. "They asked us to sit down, but they hardly spoke to us."

"Not even about the burglary," my mother added.

"And the lady was hiding something, in the folds of her sari," said my sister. "It seemed to be a small photo, a framed photo."

"Oh!" my mother exclaimed. "I didn't notice that."

"She snatched it up from that corner table as we entered," my sister explained. "I noticed it because I went in before you."

"Maybe that is why I did not see it," my mother said. "But you do notice things much more than most people."

"Good work, Rhea," my uncle said through a mouthful of food. "There seems to be a mystery there. But I will not investigate. Not when the couple is so snobbish."

My mother and sister spoke together. "They are not snobbish." And my sister added, "Just very sad."

"And anyway," my grandfather said, "nobody has asked you to investigate anything. So don't go poking your nose into other people's business." My grandfather then looked at my mother and said, "I wasn't happy about you and Rhea visiting them either."

My father, who is usually very silent at dinner, spoke up suddenly, "I think it was a very friendly thing to do," he said. "Aman told me that when he visited them later, Mr and Mrs Anand spoke of how touched they were, by your visit and your offer of help."

Dinner ended with no more words said, and I noticed how my grandfather's face was set very stern, my mother was trying not to smile, and my uncle was in a cloud of sulk.

I thought then, that I had started learning to be a noticer too, like my sister. But I still had to learn a lot. As we were clearing the table, my sister asked me in a whisper, "Neel, you won't mind if I tell you something?"

I must say I got a little irritated by her question, especially because of the whispering part so I just nodded.

"Don't get upset," my sister said quietly. "It is about Twinkle. She…She…well she is not really interested in you. You realize that, don't you?"

This was so unexpected from her that I almost dropped the dish I was holding.

"What do you mean, not interested in me?" I asked, trying not to shout. "You know how she hangs around for me in school and when I'm coming home and…"

My sister cut in. "I know all that, Neel," she said. "Everybody in school knows it. But she is just playing a game with you, can't you see?"

"What do you mean a game?" I shouted, not caring if those in the drawing room heard me. "With me?"

My sister looked sad as she said, "Yes, Neel. Twinkle is a very mixed-up girl. I think she thought that…that if you fell for her, became a friend, sort of, she would get closer to…"

"To?" I asked. "To whom?" "To Rafi."

I couldn't say anything more to my sister. I finished my part of the clearing up and went up to my room. My sister had tried to say something as I left the kitchen but I ignored her. Alone in my room, I thought of all the ways I had used to get rid of Twinkle and now…Now I had been told she was after somebody else all the time. She was just using me! I was nothing to her. I was just a pawn…It was Rafi she was interested in.

Rafi! I remember how bitter I felt. Why did I feel bitter?

I should have felt relieved. But I did feel bitter.

It took me a long time to sleep that night. At one point, I felt I should have said something to my sister, given her a hug, maybe. I got up, thinking I could do that now. But then I realized it was midnight.

I decided I would give her that hug first thing in the morning.

But the next day, the world turned upside down. Not just that day. It was almost every day after that. The world turned cartwheels without stopping.

And that is how I grew up, in an undignified, clumsy way, in a horrible hurry.

Even now, when I think of that time, my stomach goes cold. It was as if everything that had happened to me before that, was sweet and childish. Even the Twinkle problem. Then, from about the middle of February till the final exams started, me, my family and the entire colony got caught in a kind of explosion.

The first blast happened in school.

My sister had left earlier than usual that day, and I was wondering why. Then I remembered that this was the day when the new wall newspaper would be out. So I hurried up with my breakfast and rushed to school. As I reached the gates, the Tree Boy came running up to me, and pulled down my ear. "Disaster!" he whispered. "Cat...cat...apostrophe."

I pulled my ear back and snapped at him. "What is?"

Then I noticed his face. It was white, his lips dry. "You go and see," he said in a hoarse voice and ran off.

The grounds were full of groups of students, whispering to each other, some looking over their shoulder, most of them with shocked faces. I suddenly found my sister rushing up to me, with a look of, not just shock but of fear. Before I could speak, she said, "O Neel! Go and see what they have written. O god! I feel sick."

I ran into the building. The entrance hall was thick with silence except for small murmurs of "O my god", and a great many gasps. These came from the enormous group of students crowding around the notice board. Clusters of them kept breaking away and I heard some of them say, "How can anyone write this? Someone like us, someone we know?"

I pushed my way through the crowd, till I got to where I could read the board. My piece was in the middle surrounded by a sort of garland of pictures of our Indian flag, drawn with crayons and with the name of the artists written in bold capitals, all from Class 1. There was also a large picture of a lotus drawn with a compass, coloured golden, titled "Our National Flower". Besides these drawings, were pieces of writing saying, "India is the Best", "I love India because this is where I was born," and a longer article which began with the line, "India is my motherland and I love her".

But nobody was reading these pieces. What was holding everyone's attention were two or three other pieces to the left of mine. I read them quickly as I stood there, jostled all the time. I remember only some of the words. One writer said ..."they were invaders." Another said..."they are not us." A third said, "I saw people dancing when the mosque was demolished".

The name of the writer had been crossed out on all these pieces.

For the first time that I can remember, morning assembly started late that day. It was nearly ten minutes past nine, before we heard PT Ma'am's whistle. There was some chatter among the juniors but nobody among the seniors even opened their mouths. It was as if somebody had died.

We said the morning prayer, which was read out that day by Mrs D'Souza, not from the Bible but was a Sanskrit shloka. She recited it first in Sanskrit and then read the translation. It was a prayer with no names of any gods but the meaning was that we must pray for peace, that nobody should be hurt and we must wish that everybody should be happy. After that the Principal came to the mike. She looked as if she had come out of a fight but had not given up.

I still remember, almost word for word, what she said that day.

"Dear children and staff of this school that I love so much, today is one of the saddest days of my life. When we decided to start a wall newspaper where you, my dear students could express your opinions freely, it was with the intention of shaping you all to be independent thinkers. We wanted you to go out into the world, not just distinguished in academics, but as young people with minds of your own, capable of thinking outside your textbooks, wise in how you use the knowledge you have, ready to keep learning every day of your lives. These days, when our country is going through such turmoil, it seemed to us, that your young, fresh voices would give us the energy to carry on our work of making our country strong, of showing the world that we have not forgotten the message of peace and non-violence that Mahatma Gandhi taught us and for which he died. We did receive such pieces for the wall newspaper and you also saw that we received others."

Here, I remember she paused, almost stopped. Then she continued.

"We received articles from our students that we had not expected. We have put them up because we had said that this was a place where you could express your opinions, whatever those may be. So, after much debate we put up these pieces but we crossed out the names of the writers. This was done so that the writers do not face any backlash from other students, or the parents of other students. The wall newspaper shall be taken down after this, and for the time being, we shall not continue with it. It is time for your annual exams and we shall all have to start work on that."

She paused again, then said, "The opinions expressed by some students have hurt many of us. Of course we want you to be independent in your thinking, you don't all have to be Mahatma Gandhi or Martin Luther King but there is just one thing I would like you to remember. We are all different in the way we look, the food we eat, the language we speak, the gods we pray to. We are different, but these differences need not and should not divide us. Dear, beloved students, hate is corrosive, it eats us up. Accept difference with joy. That's what makes the world an exciting place."

I remember how quiet the school was that day. It was as if we had all gone through an earthquake and saw how some houses had collapsed completely, and how others were still standing, even though they were damaged. But now when I recall that day, I realize how suddenly we became suspicious of each other. It was as if we had a thief or a murderer among us and we did not know who it was.

What detecting could I do?

That evening we were all in a grey mood. I did not go out but I did give my sister the hug that I had promised myself I would. She gave me a tight hug back and asked, "You, okay? About Twinkle, I mean. I cannot think any more about what happened in school today. I feel like throwing up."

I gave her another tight hug. About Twinkle I had to be honest. "I'm alright I think," I said. "But feeling like a fool."

"That's part of growing up," she said softly. "It's hard but we have to go through it."

How is it that my sister, a year, five months and ten days younger than me, is wiser than I am? Is it a gender thing? I would have liked to talk to Ari about it but somehow I did not want to meet him that day. So I went up to the terrace and crashed the ball around a few times. It was a Friday evening I remember and we had been given a lot of revision work by all the teachers.

Revision and exams seemed to be so far away from what was happening in our minds. All that hate. Thinking of it made me sick.

Then I heard Dog barking and whining at the same time. That was funny. Was Twinkle back with her four-legged, cowardly bully? I looked over the terrace parapet and to my surprise, saw Ari. He was standing outside our house and speaking to Dog in a low voice using words I could not hear. Dog's tail was wagging furiously, he was whining, and his nose was pressed against the bars of the gate. I was about to call out when Ari suddenly looked up and waved. "See you on Sunday," he shouted and walked away quickly.

It was all very strange. I was far too confused about everything that was happening, I didn't think too much about why Ari had come to our gate and then gone away without coming in.

Over dinner that night, my sister and I told the family what had happened in school that day. I spoke some of the lines in the hate messages but I couldn't go on. Everyone stopped eating and both my sister and my mother started crying.

I should not have said those words at all. I know that now. It is just that I was not able to get them out of my mind. I remember them even now.

Why do we remember bad things much better than good things? Much longer too. My uncle changed the conversation. He did not have anything pleasant to say but at least it was not about hateful words. He told us that another journalist who had been assigned the job by his paper of secretly investigating a scam in which a top politician was allegedly involved, had gone missing, and his editors were worried.

"This is the third chap I am hearing about," my uncle said. "They are threatened, they are beaten up, even their families get threat calls. Sometimes, they just disappear."

"But how can that happen?" I asked. "The journalists are just doing their job. What about the police? They are supposed to protect everybody."

My uncle's laugh was grating. "Grow up, Neel, won't you?" he said. "This world is not rosy and sweet at all. Wrongdoers are often powerful people, or have their backing. Governments protect themselves. You think they care about citizens except when it is voting time?"

My father cut in before I could say anything.

"Do you know who the journalist is?" he asked. "I wonder if Aman can find out anything more."

"No I don't know the name," my uncle said. "The fellow who told me this, did not know. I have to find out. And anyway, what can your Aman do? He is government, isn't he?"

My father didn't reply and we finished dinner in silence. How different everything was the next day. How terrible!

Next morning, I woke up to a very strange silence in the house. It was as though there was nobody around but me. Usually Saturday mornings are noisy because there is a special breakfast being made by my father, and Pachamma comes early because she has to go somewhere or the other and needs my uncle to get up because she has to clean his room because she can't go into the kitchen because Ayya—my father—is making a mess there etc., etc.

But that Saturday, it was as if the day hadn't started yet although my watch told me it had. The sun was breaking through the clouds and even though the air had a little bite in it, I didn't feel cold enough to snuggle down in bed anymore. I went downstairs.

There was nobody in the dining room or in the kitchen but I heard a murmur of voices in the drawing room. When I went in there, I found the whole family, except my uncle but including Pachamma, gathered around the phone listening to my father speaking to somebody.

"Are you sure?" I heard him ask. Then again, "Are you sure, Aman? Is this confirmed news?"

Another burglary, I thought to myself. Where was this one now? My father was speaking in such a serious voice, that I decided a lot of stuff must have gone. Or that somebody had got attacked.

I was wrong on all counts.

My father who had been standing all this time while he was speaking, now put down the phone and without saying anything, sat down heavily on the nearest chair. I had never seen him do this before. Nor had I ever seen him suddenly look so tired and old.

"What has happened?" my grandfather asked. "What did Aman say?"

My father said in almost a whisper, "It's not good news. It is terrible. That journalist who had gone missing was Dhruv. He has been killed. His body has been found on…"

My father broke off and covered his face. My mother moved close to him and put her hand on his shoulder.

My grandfather asked in a dazed way, "Dhruv? Our Dhruv?"

My grandmother opened her mouth but no sound came. It was horrible. My father looked up at my mother and said in a whisper, "How am I to tell Viru?" Suddenly, like in a film, my uncle appeared at the doorway.

"Hey everybody!" he shouted. "Look at me! I have actually got up early. On a Saturday too! Now Pachamma cannot…"

His voice trailed off when he saw us. All frozen.

"What's the matter, folks?" he asked, a little less loudly than before. "What has happened?"

My father got up, put his arm around my uncle and led him out.

Only my sister and I managed to eat a little at breakfast that day. My grandfather did not come to the table at all. My grandmother came and sat in her chair like a statue. Pachamma had gone back to work in the kitchen when she realized that this was some bad news she did not understand. I did not understand it either. Who was Dhruv?

"Uncle's best friend all through school and college," my sister said under her breath. "They were like twins. Amma told me just now."

Suddenly my grandmother burst out, "He loved my upma. Every day, after school, he used to come home to eat my upma. I will never eat upma again, I will never look at it the rest of my life." She pushed her plate away so violently, that it fell off the table and hit the floor with a hideous clang. The upma splattered all over.

My mother went up to my grandmother and, very gently, helped her out of her chair.

"Come, Amma," she said. "You sit with Appa in the other room and I will make some hot porridge for both of you. Come."

"With lots of sugar?" my grandmother asked like a little girl.

"Yes," my mother promised. "With lots of sugar."

"Sugar is good for shocks, you know," my grandmother said as she went out with my mother.

That whole day, the house was as quiet as a class doing a maths exam. Even Pachamma did her work without the usual banging and stomping. My father and my uncle were out the whole morning. My mother sat with my grandparents, between her cooking, and talked to them. They did not respond much.

My mother spoke to my sister and me a little later in the morning. "What makes it terrible is what Mr Khan told your father, that old couple who had been robbed are Dhruv's parents. They used to live in Bengaluru when Dhruv and your uncle were together through school and college. I had never met them. Apparently Dhruv and Viru were in and out of each other's homes all the time. Afterwards, the family moved to Delhi when Mr Anand was posted there. Dhruv trained as a journalist. The two families lost contact. After all these years, when Mr Anand had retired, Dhruv had persuaded them to come back to the town where they used to live, and to get in touch with us. But they had not met us or anyone else, because they were so afraid. They never went out. Almost in hiding. Even their shopping was done by a servant boy."

"But didn't uncle know they had moved here?" I asked. "Why didn't Mr and Mrs Anand come and tell us they had moved here?"

My mother said. "They had received threats. That is why they called themselves Anand, they adopted their middle name. Mr Anand's full name is Bal Anand Murari."

Later that afternoon, my father and my uncle who had spent the whole morning with Mr and Mrs Anand brought them to our house, to meet my grandparents. My sister and I escaped to the terrace with books, and sat on upside down flower pots. Neither of us read a word.

After a long silence, my sister asked with tears in her voice, "Why did they have to kill him, Neel? He was only doing his job."

I tried to think of a proper answer, because I had been thinking of this also. "I suppose because…," I began, "because that powerful man had many guilty secrets and he didn't want them to be found out."

"Guilty secrets like making money in an illegal way?" my sister asked. "Perhaps," I said. "Or bribing people to vote for him. Or threatening them."

"Maybe even murdering somebody," my sister said, this time with anger, not sadness.

After a pause she said, "You know, Neel, our India has changed from what it used to be. It is not the India that Gandhiji and our grandparents had dreamt of. Not what our parents wanted for us to grow up in. It has become a place of hate. How can we live in a place of hate?"

I remembered what Mrs D'Souza had said to me in school and I told my sister about it.

"She is right about fear," my sister said softly. "This man with guilty secrets was afraid and so he sent threats to uncle's friend, to his parents also. Made them so afraid that they had to hide. Then either he himself or somebody he hired, killed Dhruv…"

She stopped, then said, "He was their only child, Neel. What will happen to them now?"

There are so many kinds of fear, I realized after listening to what my sister said. We, ordinary people, are afraid too. There is the small fear about passing exams, about getting bad marks. There are also somewhat bigger fears about being caught by PT Ma'am for not having a haircut or for coming to school wearing dirty white shoes. Grown-ups have much bigger fears about their work, money, about us their children, or their old parents.

But an entire country being afraid, living in fear, that was very, very different. It was like living in a science fiction story where the eggs in the fridge suddenly break out and become gigantic, carnivorous dinosaurs like in Jurassic Park. Except that the carnivorous dinosaurs now seem to be human beings. Human monsters.

I had a very bad dream that night. I dreamt that I was being chased by a huge monster with a light on its head. There was somebody riding the monster who had a loudspeaker and he was laughing at me and haranguing me for my name, asking me in a jeering way, "What is your name? Dhruv is it? Or Aman? Or by chance is it Omar? Answer. Answer." I was trying to answer and run hard at the same time, but he would not listen.

I woke up in a sweat and couldn't go back to sleep for a long time.

After those two terrible days, one in school, the other at home, the world became different. For one thing, my uncle changed completely. He became much quieter, came down for breakfast before anyone else, actually helped my mother in the kitchen till she begged him not to, because he kept asking what she wanted him to do and kept coming in Pachamma's way. He was very patient with my grandparents and also spent a lot of time with Mr and Mrs Anand.

"They have lost Dhruv," I heard him tell my father. "I have to try and be something like a son to them now."

That evening, my uncle sat very silently in the drawing room for a while. Then he said, as if speaking to himself, "You know, I lost touch with Dhruv sometime after he went to Delhi. We used to write to each other and phone once in a while. But then he got busy with his work, and I kept moving from job to job. Because of his work, he had to change his mobile number. And we lost each other. We just lost each other."

We were all very quiet. Then my mother said, "Viru, it happens to everyone. We all get busy with our own lives. We have to be so many things to so many people. Don't kick yourself."

Be a son. Be a father. Be a daughter or a mother. Be a student. Be a teacher. Be a friend. How many different things we all are. How many different parts we play! Do we change our behaviour and the way we speak, with each part?

I remember once in class when Miss Swami scolded one of my class fellows for speaking in "bad" English with our Hindi teacher.

"Why were you speaking like that?" she asked him. "Did you suddenly forget all your English grammar?"

"But, Ma'am," he said, "I don't need to speak proper English with the Hindi teacher. I only have to speak in good Hindi with her. And in proper English with you."

That Sunday, I did not feel like going to F block to practice football moves with Ari. I don't know why, it all seemed useless, a waste of time. Then I got a big surprise! Who should come to our house, and ring the bell, but Ari himself! When my mother called me downstairs, I had been half afraid it would be Twinkle. But it was Ari with a new football under his arm, and full of smiles and charm. My decision not to touch a football dissolved like a soap bubble.

"You don't have to come all the way to our part of town," he said after the "hellos". "We can play right here."

"But our ground is always full of chatting ladies and little children," I protested. "No problem," he said. "They will melt away."

And to my astonishment, they did. All of them. I don't know what he said to them, but they did melt away and with smiles and some of the children with a salute.

We practiced some terrific moves and I found that my aim had improved tremendously and I got the ball through the goal posts, two straggly bushes, four times even though Ari was the goalie!

After my fourth "goal" though, Ari abruptly stopped and said, "That's all for today, Neel. I had promised the original inhabitants that we will give back their land in half an hour."

"But it's not half an hour yet," I said. I wanted to play some more. "And anyway, the original inhabitants are not around."

But Ari had already picked up the ball and was opening the gate to our house. When we went in, I found my mother had laid the table as if we had a very important guest who had come for tea.

She smiled when she saw us. "O good," she said. "Rhea is also back after her cycle ride. You two have a wash and then come and sit down. You must be hungry."

We were hungry and I was really happy. I kept talking about my four goals and my mother asked a lot of questions about football and why the film was called "Bend it like Beckham". I had never thought my mother was interested in football. My mother had made dhokla and got a cake and Ari talked and ate as if he had known us for years. Only my sister was very quiet. She finished eating rather quickly and excused herself, saying she had a lot of revision to finish.

"Shucks!" Ari said. "I forgot it's exam time for you guys. I better leave."

"You must come again," my mother told him. "You must come and tell us all about yourself. Today the conversation seemed to be about us the whole time."

"Certainly." Ari spoke as if he was of the same age as my mother. "And you must promise to give me as excellent a meal as this one."

My mother laughed and said she would. As I went up to the door to see Ari off, I heard my grandmother call out, "Who is that good looking boy I just saw?" she asked from the drawing room. She and my grandfather had been sitting there all afternoon, looking through old photograph albums.

My mother went in and told her that Ari was my football friend. "Next time," I heard my grandmother say, "I want to meet him. His voice is just like Dhruv's."

After the sadness of the week, that Sunday evening felt to me like an oasis in a very dry, dusty desert. But again, I was wrong. It had not been an oasis for everybody at the table that day. I realized this so much later. As usual.

School went on in its routine way the following week. Everyone was in exam mode, and in a way, it was a good thing because it stopped us from thinking of what we had read on the last wall newspaper. That notice board had been taken away, and yet, whenever I went past the blank wall, I felt a sickness in my stomach. How could people think like that?

Meanwhile, the teachers gave us test after test, and we went around like zombies. Some fellows even started mumbling chemistry formulae under their breath during recess and lunch time. It was weird.

What with all that happened at home and at school, I had forgotten all about being a detective. When I thought about it, I actually felt very silly. How could I, with no training, no idea about what I was supposed to do, how could I catch a gang of thieves? Possibly rather dangerous thieves. That was a job for the police. It was better I concentrated on my exams. I suddenly wanted to be the best at something, and not just dream about it. So I decided I would even give up my football practice till the exams were over. After all, it would just be for a few weeks.

Then something very, very weird happened, a really weird thing. I think it was one or two days after that football practice with Ari, when I was woken up by a loud conversation outside our front door. I looked out of my window and I saw my father and my uncle talking to a man wearing a guard's uniform. It was he who was doing most of the talking using his hands a lot. I noticed in the light above the door, that he had cuts on one side of his face and neck. At one point I heard my father say that the man should be taken to a doctor for a tetanus shot and I heard my uncle agree and then add, "We'll go to the police after that."

I could not listen in anymore because I had to get ready for school, and, anyway, the conversation below stopped. I hurried up with my bath and wore my uniform, and then I ran down with my schoolbag, hanging half open. My sister was already at breakfast. I heard my father say, "Yes. You should tell them. They are old enough now." Then the front door banged shut and my mother came in, looking unusually tense.

"Neel, Rhea," she said as she sat down at the table. "I have to tell you about something rather serious. I am sure you heard the commotion outside just now. That was Paras who was talking. He works in your father's office but something happened to him here, in our colony, that has made him very agitated."

Apparently, the night before, Paras had been asked by his agency to be on duty at a house in Block C because the regular guard there had some emergency at home to attend to. It seems Paras had come on duty around 10 p.m. The regular guard had left immediately after telling Paras not to disturb the people in the house, who were early sleepers. So after checking that the doors and windows were all shut, Paras sat in the guard's chair at the gate. Now Block C overlooks the non-playing fountain in the centre of our colony. The horrible, green pool of stagnant water around the base of this fountain stinks so much that nobody goes anywhere near it. Many people in the colony, like my parents, have tried to clean up this place but so far, that has not happened. Anyway, what Paras said was that, because he was feeling sleepy around dawn, he had been walking about a little on the road outside the house to stay awake. Suddenly, somebody pushed him from behind and he fell. He was not much hurt but it took him a little time to get up. Then he saw a figure in black at the fountain, throwing a bundle into the green pool. It seems Paras shouted out, but the figure did not turn. It glided off and vanished.

"Nobody else knows about this, because Paras came straight to your father as soon as it was light," my mother said, as she finished the strange story. "So I would like you both to keep it to yourselves. Your father and I feel that you are both grown up and should be treated almost like adults. That is why I have told you all this."

"You mean this is not a simple ghost story?" my sister asked. "There is something more to it."

"Yes, Rhea," my mother replied. "Paras was pushed to the ground. He was just lucky that he did not hit his head or break any bones. That was no ghost. It was a human being with strong arms who struck him."

"What did Paras mean by saying that this ghost or blank figure or whatever 'glided' away?" I asked.

"We asked him that too," said my mother. "Paras is convinced this was a ghost. He says that it had no feet and it went off without touching the ground. It vanished in the blink of an eye is how he described it."

"So what did this 'ghost' throw into that stinking pool?" was my next question.

"Your father and uncle have gone to the police with Paras," my mother said. "I suppose we'll know something by the end of the day."

School felt doubly dull after this. I tried not to think of what might be in that dirty pool. Could it be a body? Or part of a body? My sister and I had been told not to speak about it to anyone, and that was very difficult too. Not so much for me because I really did not have any close friend. But my sister had many, especially a girl called Jana, with whom she goes cycling. I saw my sister sitting with Jana at lunchtime, trying to listen to something her friend was saying. I did not feel my sister was paying much attention though. That day, of all days, when I wanted to be left alone to think, one of Twinkle's brothers came up and reminded me about the "lyric" I had to write. By the way, the entire Banjo family, including Twinkle, now wore spectacles.

"We will open the club after the exams," the Banjo boy said. "And we want to start with your lyric, okay?" Before I could ask him anything, or even before I got his name right, he scooted off. He vanished.

And then, when I was about to rush out of the gates after school, I felt a tug at my shirt sleeve.

"Remember," a hoarse voice said, "a tall boy with spectacles".

"Okay, okay," I mumbled irritably and pulled away from the Tree Boy. I raced down the road, football practice with Ari really helped me. I sped down wondering whether to go straight to the fountain or go home first.

"Better to go home," said my sister's voice behind me, panting a little. "Amma will tell us."

My mother was looking very troubled when we went in. But she wouldn't say anything, till we had taken off our shoes and washed our hands. Then she sat down at the dining table and finally told us what the "ghost" had thrown into the fountain pool. And what she said was perhaps the weirdest part of the whole, strange story.

My mother told us that what the police fished out of the water was a large, cloth bundle in which there was a plastic bag full of cash, another plastic bag with silver cups, and a large silk bag containing jewellery. "Antique jewellery," my mother added.

"All the things that were stolen!" my sister whispered. "The Doongaji sisters' jewellery!"

"And the Banjo parents' silver cups!" I said. "But the cash came from where?"

My sister said softly, "That must be money from some of the houses they had burgled."

"Well, the police have not yet confirmed that what the bundle contained is the stolen stuff," my mother said. "They have asked the Doongaji sisters and Mr and Mrs Bhonjo to go to the police station to look at the items."

After a pause, she added, "Mr Anand is not in a position to go yet." We fell silent.

Then my sister asked, "Any news about the so called ghost?"

My mother shook her head. "But there's something else I have to tell you both," she said in a low voice. She paused, then said, "The police have arrested Pachamma!"

"What!" my sister and I almost shouted together. "Pachamma?"

My mother rubbed her eyes. "Yes," she replied. "She was here working in the kitchen when the police came. She saw them and tried to run out through the back door. But the policewoman caught her at the gate. She went screaming. All the neighbours came out and saw her being taken away."

Neither Rhea nor I could say anything. Amma had tears in her eyes. Both of us went up and gave her a tight hug. What else could we do? There were so many questions I wanted to ask, but it was clear that Amma would not be able to answer any of them. The police had not told her anything except that they were taking Pachamma for questioning.

"But they had brought handcuffs," my mother said. "It was an arrest."

We were all very quiet that whole evening. My grandparents continued to look through old photo albums, searching for pictures that showed Dhruv. My father and uncle had still not returned. Rhea and I helped Amma with the washing up and sweeping under the dining table. Then she shooed us upstairs to study. I tried to, but found it difficult because there was a lot of noise outside. We could hear mobikes and vans tearing around at great speed. Our phone kept ringing and I could hear my mother getting more and more irritated with each call. Finally, I heard her shout at one caller, saying, "No. I have no sound bites or sound eats to give you. Stop calling this number." I had never heard my mother shout like that before so I came out of my room, letting go that hateful revision, and started going down the stairs. My sister came out too. Amma appeared at the foot of the stairs. "Sorry children," she called up to us. "Those were media people trying to get an interview. God knows how they had our number but I have now disconnected the landline and asked your father to contact me on the mobile if he needs to. You two go back to your books."

We returned to our rooms, but it was impossible to study. When the phone stopped ringing, the front door bell started. There was ringing and there was knocking. There were loud voices.

"Ma'am, ma'am! We'll take only one minute...Just answer, Ma'am! That woman who has been arrested...Ma'am? Sir? Do you suspect anybody...Did you ever see the ghost?"

My mother did not open the door but the voices became so loud that my grandmother came out of the drawing room and started yelling, "Who are you? Do you have any news of Dhruv? Speak. Speak out."

My sister and I shot out of our rooms, and rushed downstairs. By then, my mother was already out of the kitchen, persuading my grandmother to go back into the drawing room.

"Neel," my mother said when she saw me, "just see what you can do to get these pests away."

My mouth went dry, my legs were shaking. But I had to do it.

I put the chain on the door and then opened it just enough to peep out. There was a large group of them outside, men and women, some with mikes, others holding cameras, many with pens and notebooks. Their shouting stopped when they saw me. I swallowed my nervousness, then I said, without raising my voice, "Listen, I know you are doing your job. But we have just heard that one of our close relatives has died. My grandparents are very old and are finding it difficult to cope with news. So please help us by going away."

There was a moment's silence. Then a woman wearing a cap, the wrong way around, said, "Right o young man. You take care of them." And then, just as if she had given an order, the whole lot of them turned, some of them grumbling, and walked away, leaving the road in blessed silence. I closed the door, stunned at what I had done.

Amma and Rhea were standing behind me, smiling and crying at the same time. They hugged me tight and then my grandfather came up, his hand stretched out to shake mine warmly. "Good work, my boy," he said. "Good work."

My grandmother followed him, saying in her quavering voice, "He is as brave as Dhruv."

For a moment, I felt I was a hero, at least to my family.

The paper was full of our colony news the next morning. It was not on the front page but on what is called the "city page". There was nothing about me but there was a lot about the ghost and the mysterious packet and the "loot" found in it. There were interviews with people who lived in our colony but we did not know them. One lady said the colony had bad "vaastu" and many bad things were happening here, including a horrible music club which the police had closed. Another lady said she had stopped going for morning walks and evening walks, because of all the burglaries and was going only for "noon walks". An old gentleman said the whole trouble with the colony was the vast number of "uncontrolled, foul dogs". The reporter had spelt the word "foul" with a "w" and anyway, the old gentleman must have been talking about a certain dog, an "uncontrolled", growling creature. But the most interesting interview was with a person who said he had seen the ghost many times and it was the ghost of Kempegowda, the founder of Bengaluru. This man said he had scientific proof of this. According to him, the ghost appears only in the winter when a certain bean called "avarekai" that grows only in Karnataka, is harvested. The ghost can be seen eating these beans boiled, according to this man whose photograph was also on the page.

The city's TV channel showed "our" story too. There were pictures of the fountain and the now dry and cleaned pool. Their reporter was able to track down Paras and interview him but he was so nervous, that we could not understand what he said. The TV reporter also interviewed old Babu, the cobbler who sits at one end of the market and can repair anything, from a punctured football to an electric kettle. Babu was very scornful of the "ghost" and told the reporter that it was all just "drama" and that it was a greedy human thief who enjoyed fooling people. Then the channel showed the whole colony, saying it was a fine place and had many distinguished residents. The channel also had a shot of our school calling it the neighbourhood school, well known for its academic record. At this point, they showed a picture of students in a classroom, busy writing. As the camera moved, the reporter commented that the TV crew was not allowed to interview any of the students because they were all writing their board exams.

I could not make out what school this picture showed because the students were not wearing our uniform and anyway, the written exams for the boards had not started. The TV reporter went on to say that she could not get an interview with the police or with the people whose houses were burgled. "Thank god," my mother muttered. The reporter ended by saying that the police had made only one arrest so far, and then she asked, "Is this too little, too late?"

Afterwards, Rhea and I discussed what exactly the reporter meant by asking that question, but we could find no answer.

A few days later, we overheard our father telling our mother that the police investigation was almost near its end and there would be many more arrests soon. In the meanwhile, my mother had got another maid, introduced by Mrs Raj. The new maid's name was Farida. She was very quiet and kept her head covered even when she was working in the kitchen. After she finished work on the first day, she asked my mother whether she could learn English from her. My mother was so happy that she bought a whole lot of books and started lessons the next day. When my grandmother heard this, she wanted to teach Farida too. So one day when I came back from school, I saw all three at the dining table, Farida bending over a book, trying to listen to two teachers talking at the same time.

My mother was helping her to use simple words like "come" and "go" while my grandmother was telling her a long, complicated story about how she taught English to her aunt who had never gone to school.

"Yes, yes," my grandmother was saying as I went into the dining room, "I also taught her those things. I told her, 'Say after me in English, "I go".' But she refused. Refused and refused. Why I asked. She said in our language, 'I will never say "I go". I will say, "I will go and come"'. After some days, she stopped my teaching. She said English was a rude language, spoken by the jailers of our country. I agreed with that. So I stopped."

It was around this time, that I noticed that my sister was not talking about Rafi as much as she used to, nor was she going to his house as often. Earlier, she would even come home with him from school, now she waited for me. I liked this very much and one day, I told her. She hugged me, a little clumsily, because of our bags, and said, "I like it too." Then after a pause, she said softly, "You must have noticed I don't meet Rafi like I used to."

I said I had noticed. "Don't you want to know why?" she asked in a teasing sort of way.

"Do you want to tell me?" I asked her back.

She became serious. "Of course I do," she said. "The thing is everyone in school was talking about how Twinkle was chasing you and how you were trying to get rid of her."

I was taken aback. "You mean people notice all these things?" I asked. "And talk about it?"

"Yes," she said. "There is a lot of gossip that goes on in school, a lot. Mostly boyfriend girlfriend stuff. Also about teachers' pets and all that."

"So they talked in front of you about me and...?"

"Oh!" she said with some anger. "They came up to me and told me. They were making fun of you, some of them, saying you had become so swollen headed after Mrs D'Souza made you a hero on Republic Day, that you did not even realize what Twinkle was doing."

"Using me as a pawn," I said. Yes, a bit bitterly.

Rhea was quiet. Then she said, "I began to think about what they might be saying about me. And...and Rafi. That made me feel sick. I talked to Amma. She said what I felt about Rafi was quite okay, it happens, there is nothing wrong with it. But maybe I should wait before I take all this seriously. I should study, pass out of school, decide on a career before…"

We had reached home by this time. We stood at the gate and suddenly I saw my sister as the little girl whose hand I held, as she walked to school with me the first time. She had grown up so much. So wisely.

"You stopped seeing Rafi for my sake too," I said. "Thank you."

She was solemn for a moment and then she giggled. It was a lovely sound; I hadn't heard it for a long time. We walked in and to my astonishment, found Ari sitting in the drawing room talking merrily to my grandparents and my mother.

He turned when he heard us coming in. "Hi, Neel," he said, looking at my sister. "I came to check on how you are getting on with your revision."

My sister slipped out of the room and left me to answer his rather stupid question. "Oh, okay," I mumbled and didn't know what else to say. My mother got up saying, "I better get your snack ready. You sure you won't eat anything Ari?"

Ari shook his head, his smile had faded a little. My grandmother who had broken off some story in the middle, started off again. "…I told him then he can't have his way all the time. He was growing thinner minute by minute, you know. I mean Dhruv, not my son who always has a good appetite…"

My grandmother paused to catch her breath, and Ari got up hurriedly. "I must be off," he said. He bowed to my grandparents and came out of the room with me. "Okay, Neel," he muttered. "All the best." He left without taking leave of my mother who, surprisingly, was not in the kitchen.

She was upstairs with my sister. I saw them when I went up. They were sitting on the bed and my mother was holding Rhea in her arms. Rhea was crying. "It's alright, my darling," my mother was murmuring. "I'm glad you told me. It will be alright."

Then my mother looked up and saw me. "I'll be down in a minute, Neel," she said. "You go take off your shoes and wash your hands." Then she gave a very small shake of her head. I was not to ask any questions.

Rhea was very subdued the whole evening. Later, after dinner, I heard my father talk to her for a long time sitting in her room. At one point, I thought I heard my father say something like "…talk to Neel" and my sister saying "No" quite loudly. Now that I know what this was all about, I sometimes wish Rhea had talked to me the way she had told me about Rafi. But I'm not sure. All of us have secrets, some big, some quite silly and we don't like to talk about them, especially to our parents, I don't know why. I am really glad that my sister did tell my mother everything, before all that happened later. All the terrible things.

It was nearly the end of February. Exam fever and exam fear were both very high at school. Senior students who were doing their boards had already finished most of their practicals in another school and came in groups to tell their teachers how they had done. Some looked pale and tired, others more confident. "It's much the same every year," I overheard a senior teacher tell her colleague. "Our children go through hell and then they come out with distinctions. Why do they have to be tortured like this? Can't we have a kinder system?"

Rafi couldn't be seen at all, he was one of the board types and he was also getting ready for a whole lot of entrance exams. Even Dog had learnt, or been sternly taught, to be quiet and barked very softly when he saw us as if he did not know us well but the furious wagging of his tail did not quite match the bark.

Rhea brought home her friend Jana, with whom she goes cycling, one afternoon, because they wanted to study together. I don't know how much studying they did, I heard them talk a lot but my sister looked much calmer that evening. It was while we were setting the table for dinner, that there was a ring at the door. Since both my father and my uncle had keys to the front door, we wondered who it might be. It was Mrs Raj who almost shoved my mother out of the way in her hurry to get in and close the door.

"Spies!" she gasped, trying to get her breath back. "Spies are everywhere. I am talkeeng softly only because Neel and Rhea are doing studies. No? Then I am telleeng you beeg news. Bhery beeg news. You habe to do all ironing yourself. Uph! This jeans and all so bheri tough. So much."

Since in her excitement Mrs Raj's accent was difficult to understand, my mother made her sit down and gave her a glass of water.

"Why should I do the ironing, Mrs Raj?" my mother asked. "Farida now takes the clothes to Sundar herself and brings them back also."

"Those days all gone," Mrs Raj moaned. She gulped down the water, then in the most dramatic fashion, she announced, "Arrested. Sundar ees in jail."

At that precise moment, my father and my uncle appeared at the door to the dining room. Who said such things happen only in films?

They were both looking tired and upset. My mother looked at them with a question she did not have to ask.

"Yes, it is true," my father said. "Sundar has been arrested and a few others as well. But how did you know about it, Mrs Raj? It happened just a little while ago."

Mrs Raj spoke with the pride that some people have when they are first with the news.

"Mr Raj was taking his evening walk," she said. "And he haard the market people saying something and all. So he went to the roundabout and saw no Sundar. Only his gaadi was there and some police people. So he asked thaym."

"But what has Sundar done?" my mother asked. "First Pachamma, now Sundar…"

My father did not reply. He shook his head and went off murmuring that he had to make a phone call. It was my uncle who said, "The police did not tell us much. Just said that he was operating some kind of network and Pachamma and a few others were part of it."

"What network?" Mrs Raj demanded.

But my uncle had no more information to give and finally Mrs Raj left, saying she was sure the papers would give her the "full news tomorrow morning itself". After she had gone, and after we had finished dinner, my father told us more. He started by saying that this was very confidential information he was giving us.

"You are not to share it with anyone," he said. "I am trusting you about this, don't let me down."

When he said it like that, I started feeling guilty as if I had already opened my mouth and given out the information. How stupid of me!

"You've just heard that Sundar and a few others have been arrested," my father went on. "It seems Sundar was the one who was giving the thieves the information about which house in the colony had suddenly become empty. We all know that in our colony, it is very rare for a house to be totally without people, somebody or the other is always in. And in each case of burglary in the last few months, the house became unexpectedly empty and the thieves moved in immediately. How did they know?"

"How did Sundar know there was nobody in the house?" asked my mother. "He never leaves his ironing cart, he is always there."

My father paused for a minute. Then he said, "That is where maids like Pachamma came into the picture. There is a whole network of part-time maids, working in different houses, who kept their eyes and ears open and reported to Sundar as soon as they found out."

"Oh my god!" my mother whispered. "Pachamma worked in so many houses. She also has relatives, so many of them, working in the colony."

"But how did they tell Sundar so quickly?" my sister asked. "You mean they ran that fast?"

It was my uncle who answered. "Sundar had two mobile phones," he said. "One was for people like us who called him to get their clothes collected. The other one he kept hidden under his cart. This one was set to beep and to carry a message."

"The house number?" I asked.

"Quite right, Neel," my father said half smiling. "The number and the block."

"Do you mean to say," my mother said in a tone of amazement, "that women like Pachamma were sending these messages? She cannot read or write. She was never sent to school."

"But she is an intelligent woman," my uncle said. "She was taught the English alphabet from A to H and…"

"And she is numerate, she knows numbers!" my sister said softly.

"That's right, she does," my mother agreed. "She knows exactly how much I pay her every month. In fact, she is very good at keeping accounts."

"But how is it that she got arrested before Sundar and the others?" my sister asked. "Did she slip up somewhere?"

"Yes, she did," my uncle answered. "You see, these women had been given red cotton scarves to clip on to the clothes lines to confirm that those houses were empty. This was an added precaution, in case the gang went into the wrong house. And Pachamma…"

"…tied that scarf over her head one evening," I said. "I saw her. It was a very cold evening."

"That was it!" my uncle said, beaming at me. "The police had been very puzzled by finding a red scarf on the clothes lines of many burgled houses. This scarf did not belong to anyone in the house. So why was it there?"

"Then somebody saw Pachamma wearing that red scarf?" my sister asked.

It was my father who replied this time. "That's right," he said. "One of the police detectives was chatting casually to a few children in D block, asking if anyone of them had seen a red scarf anywhere. He pretended he had lost his. Then one little chap piped up and said he had seen Pachamma wearing one. A really smart boy, this one. He knew her name and where she works…Apparently, he wants to be a detective!"

"That's the Tree Boy!" I exclaimed and then I had to explain why I called him that. My father chuckled. "Well," he said. "I'm sure all trees are as sharp-eyed as he is. If only they could speak too."

For a moment, I wished the police detective had spoken to me, then my father would have praised me for being sharp-eyed. Then I told myself that I was being stupid, I could still impress my father in other ways.

So I asked, "When Sundar got the message, what did he do?"

"He sent the same message out to the chief of the gang, the ringleader," my father said. "That person then sent it to the gang members."

"So Sundar was not the ringleader?" my mother asked.

"O no!" my father replied. "He was just the link between the maids and the gang, mostly unemployed, young men, who committed the actual burglary. The ringleader is the one who planned the whole operation, organized it and kept it going."

"And made the payments I suppose," my mother said.

"Yes," my father said, getting up. "This person was a generous paymaster, the police say. Everything that was stolen was sold and the money equally distributed."

"But who is this person?" my sister asked. "Hasn't the Inspector found out yet?"

But my father was already out of the room, and my uncle merely shrugged his shoulders.

Did they both know even then? And wouldn't tell us? I haven't yet had the courage to ask them this.

What my father and uncle told us that evening, was not easy to forget nor easy to remember. How could it be easy after finding out that people we have known for so many years, had actually been thieves? Or been part of a gang of thieves. They did not go into houses and steal anything but they helped the gang with information. They took the money too. So they were thieves, they were crooks. They would have to go to jail.

How could I imagine that somebody I knew since I was small was now in jail?

"Pachamma used to be very very honest, you know," my mother said to us at breakfast the next morning. "She did not take even a spoon from our house, not a rupee note. You," she said to my uncle, "leave money all over the place but you never found anything missing."

Then she added, "But something happened in the last six or eight months. Someone showed her how she could make easy money."

"Make easy money, without dirtying her hands," my father said. "She apparently told the police that all she did was to exchange news, passing on some gossip and what was wrong with that?"

"What about the red scarf?" my sister asked. "That was not just news or gossip."

"That, according to her," my uncle said, "was even more innocent. She was just drying her scarf in the sun. Did she have to get permission for that, she asked the police. She screamed at them apparently."

My mother seemed to feel that Pachamma's bad behaviour was, in some way, her fault.

"Why has she become like this?" she kept asking. "She was so different when she first came."

Everyone changes I realized. Everything also changes. Things changed the next day itself. Changed in such an unexpected, horrible way.

MARCH

I remember every moment of that afternoon even now. I know I have a good memory but what happened that afternoon, I cannot rub out from my mind. It was so terrible, so awful.

It was the last day of revisions. The exams were to start the following week. Rhea and I were coming home from school, feeling very full of re-re-re revision. I was telling my sister that I wished I could throw all my textbooks and notes into the Bay of Bengal, when I heard thudding footsteps from behind us, thudding, urgent footsteps and a gasping cry of "Help! Please help!"

We both turned and there was Tree Boy, his face a mask of horror and his lips dry. "Please help!" he gasped. Behind him was Jumper, as horror-stricken, also moaning, "Help! Please!"

"What is it?" I asked. "What drama is this?

My sister shushed my irritation. "What is it?" she asked much more gently.

The Tree Boy turned to her gratefully. "They are attacking him!" he stammered between breaths. "Tall boy with glasses. I told you about him. I told you," he added, turning to me.

As usual, my sister caught on instantly. "Where?" she asked. The two boys pointed towards A block. "Behind the Walker's

Park," Jumper said and sat down heavily on the road, school bag and all.

Rhea and I ran, with the Tree Boy following us, still repeating weakly, "Help. Please help!"

We reached the park. We heard the sounds. The horrible sounds of thrashing and the words, "Go back you b…! Go back to your bloody country, you swine!"

We turned the corner, and there in a shady, deserted part of the road, were two or three boys in our school uniform, beating and kicking somebody tall who had fallen down, his school shirt bloody, his face bleeding, his glasses on the road, broken.

"Stop!" I yelled. "Stop it! Rhea, go, call Dad!" I threw down my bag and ran towards the group. One of the boys turned, lunged at me, and punched my face, muttering more foul words. I hit him back. One of the other boys came towards me, his fist tight and ready, but before he could use it on me, somebody came flying up and crashed into him—somebody whose foot speed I knew so well.

Everything was a blur after that. I felt dizzy, I felt like vomiting, I tasted blood in my mouth, the trees were whirring around me, I could hear a storm of hitting and kicking and boxing and bad words and then…a police whistle and Rhea, her eyes full of tears, wiping my face with a hanky that smelt of potato curry.

It was not a bad dream. It happened. It was the Sports Captain, "the tall boy with spectacles" who, with his friends, had attacked Rafi. They hated him because he was a brilliant student, they hated him because girls liked him, but worst of all, they hated him because they thought he was a Muslim, he had a Muslim name.

I got to know all this only much later. After the Tree Boy got the police to the scene, the fight stopped of course. But there were three people who were very seriously injured. Rafi's left arm was fractured and he had severe bruises on his face. Luckily, his glasses fell off, otherwise his eyes may have got cut. The Sports Captain had a broken rib. Ari was the one who was most badly injured. One of the other boys had hit him on the head, with a stone. Ari had fallen unconscious. I was hurt too but not much. My lips had got cut and my left ear was swollen. What made me really sick was the hate I had felt that afternoon from those three boys. Such anger. Such hate. Their faces were tight and stiff as if they had never smiled in their lives and never laughed. Never would.

What had made them like this?

The day after the fight, the Principal and Mrs D'Souza came home and had a long chat with my parents and grandparents. They had brought chocolates, apparently for Rhea and me. But when my grandmother saw the box with its gift wrapping, she said, "O! How did you know it is my birthday today? Thank you. Dhruv always remembered my birthday, you know."

Later in the afternoon, when my grandmother was asleep, my mother brought the box to us. My grandmother had not even opened it. That was when I realized that my grandmother was not well.

Luckily, I did not miss any exams. I asked my father how the others were doing. He told me that both Ari and the Sports Captain were in hospital, and in intensive care units. The police had placed a guard to keep an eye on them. Ari was slipping in and out of consciousness and was not allowed any visitors. But his parents had been informed and they were on their way.

By then, the XII board written papers had begun, and Rafi, his arm in a sling, had gone to the exam centre in a cab, with his father. Rhea and I saw him as we were setting out for school. His mother was standing anxiously at the gate, her lips moving; she must have been saying a prayer. Dog was at her feet, looking anxious too, whining. We heard Rafi telling his father, "I'm going alone for the next paper, Baba."

Then he saw us and waved with his good arm. "The injured war hero!" he said, grinning. "Wish me luck."

Suddenly, I liked him enormously.

It was my English exam that day, our first paper. Everyone behaved like robots controlled by an alien device. Nobody spoke in an ordinary way, they only compared notes and kept repeating grammar terms. Is this what exams do to us? Turn us into machines? I thought about this because though I had come to school with a swollen lip and a strip of plaster across my ear, nobody seemed to notice. Only the Tree Boy gave me a thumbs up and the Jumper jumped when he saw me. One of my class fellows asked in passing, "Been in a fight?" Before I could say "yes" quite truthfully, he had joined his notes-comparing friends. Obviously, the Principal had made sure the fight had not become public knowledge.

Was this a good thing? I don't know. How many things should be kept away from us? Does it help us to know? Or not to know?

However, many of the teachers came up to pat me on the shoulder and asked me to take care. Miss Swami did too. And Miss Mary of course. Mrs Guhan, my class teacher took very special care that my desk was close to hers, in case I needed any sort of help, of the medical kind. I was fine though, except for a bit of a headache. I was a little more upset that nobody asked me what had happened. The whole thing had been hushed up, I realized. But I did feel cheated.

I had to be my own hero.

Meanwhile, my grandmother got worse day by day. Rhea and I were busy with our exams but even we could see how she had changed. One day, at dinner, she screamed at my uncle, when he tried to help her out of her chair. "Who are you? Don't touch me. I will call the police." Then she started yelling for Dhruv.

"Dhruv, come soon. The upma is getting cold. Come quickly. Hurry up."

Another time, I woke up to hear my grandmother shouting for coffee in the middle of the night. "I want coffee! Coffee!" she wailed. "My mouth is dry. Why can't anybody give me coffee?"

My mother, then my father, tried to calm her down. It seemed to take a long time. I went back to sleep at some point.

Strangely, as Rhea and I walked to school and back, there were two things we did not talk about: 1. That terrible fight 2. Our grandmother.

We talked a lot about other things, how we had done the exam, how difficult or easy the paper was, what the teachers had said, what our classmates had chatted about etc., etc. But we never brought up the fight and never mentioned our grandmother.

Maybe we were afraid.

Then one day, just after my Hindi paper, which I had not done well, Rhea and I saw an ambulance outside our gate and the doctor's grey car. The door was open and we rushed in. My mother came out of our grandparents' room, her face dark with worry.

"Rhea, Neel," she whispered, "take off your shoes and wash your hands quickly, then come and see your grandmother. She fell in the bathroom and hurt her back. She has to go to hospital."

When we went into our grandparents' room we found it full of people. My grandfather was sitting in a chair at her bedside. My father and my uncle were standing next to him, along with the doctor. I saw that there were also two or three people wearing white overalls and masks, waiting near the window. My grandmother was speaking to the doctor in great gasps. "I know what has happened, Doc," she was saying. She tried to laugh but couldn't. "I should not have gone to the bathroom on my own, I know," she went on. Then stopped. "I was too proud," she muttered after a pause. "Always was. Too proud. Higgledy-piggledy and proud."

"Alright, Doc," she said after another pause. "I agree to go to the hospital. But I will never reach there, you know. And I won't go without seeing my grandchildren."

My mother pushed us forward. "Here they are, Amma," she said softly. "Here are Neel and Rhea."

My sister and I went up to the bed. I felt a little frightened. I didn't know what I was supposed to do. But my grandmother made it so easy. She took our hands in both her own, and said, "Neel, Rhea, I am going. Take care of your grandfather. Take care of our India. Bless you both."

Her hands dropped away. Rhea bent and kissed her cheek. I did too. My grandmother was muttering something that sounded like "Inqilab…" but I could not hear properly. The doctor said in an urgent tone, "She is fading," and pushed us away. The ambulance men rushed forward and within minutes the room was empty except for our grandfather, our mother and us.

My grandmother never reached the hospital. She died on the way.

The next few days were so full of chaos that I don't remember them properly. I only remember telling my mother that I did not want to see the body when it came home because my grandmother was not there anymore. But Amma asked me gently just to place some flowers at her feet. I did that, so did Rhea. Many people from the colony and people I did not know, came and went. I remember seeing the Inspector and the Doongaji sisters. Mrs Raj went in and out, bringing us food and "spasal" coffee for my grandfather. It was difficult to study. Finally, Dhruv's parents took Rhea and me to their place "to be away from everything for a while". We went with our books and tried to study but it was difficult. The Anands were very kind and put on a cartoon channel for us!

I was glad we were with them. Mrs Raj had apparently wanted us to be at her place. But since Rafi still had two more board papers to study for, my mother did not want us to disturb him. Anyway, being next door to our house would not have made me feel alright. I suppose Rhea also would have found it difficult.

Flowers and tears and silences, my grandfather sitting in his chair without a word, without a tear, as if he had become a piece of stone, my father and uncle with shaven heads, my mother breaking into sobs every now and then, the smell of grief everywhere. I don't know how Rhea and I managed to give our exams. But we did. We did not miss a single one.

After the last exam, when we came home to a calm, silent house, Rhea and I met our father at the door. He was waiting for us. He put his arms around us and brought us in.

"I wanted to tell you both that I am very proud of you," he said. "Your grandmother always told me you were two of the best human beings she knew." Here he stopped, then said, "She was right."

The house felt strange. The rest of us were all there, and yet, without her sitting in her rocking chair, the rooms seemed empty. Every time I went downstairs, I expected to see her, to hear her chatter and her sudden, unexpected laugh. I never thought I would miss her so much.

Then came the final blow. I hope final for some time at least. Nothing made my stomach curl as this one did, not the horrible things on the wall newspaper, not the fight, not even my grandmother's absence. What happened before the terrible month of March ended, and what I had to swallow, was worse than anything that had come before.

It was also a horrible head blow because I never, never expected it. How on earth could I have?

It was two days after our final papers. Rhea and I were at home, telling each other that we would not look at our school books again for as long as we lived. Rhea's friend Jana who had dropped in, laughed and said, "What about when we all go up to the next class?"

Next class! Class 10 for me. I almost fell down when I thought of that.

After Jana left, Rhea brought out the Scrabble board and all of us, my parents and uncle too, sat in the drawing room with my grandfather. He had become more and more silent after my grandmother died and also a bit strange. For example, he would not let my mother take away the rocking chair which was always where my grandmother sat. That evening, I remember, he was sitting with his hand on the arm of the chair and rocking it slightly, as if he was rocking a baby to sleep. Rhea and I were trying to look up the meaning of the word "anent" when the doorbell rang. My uncle jumped up.

"I'll get it," he said. "Must be the Anands." It wasn't.

Three people walked in with my uncle. Three people I had not expected in a thousand years. There was Ari, his head almost entirely covered in a huge, white bandage. He had a slight limp too. Behind him were two rather tall people, a lady and a gentleman who introduced themselves as "Arvind's parents". They both spoke as if they were used to being listened to and used to being obeyed. Somewhat like our school Principal.

My father said "hello" and introduced himself and us. Ari's parents gave us all a sharp look while sitting down. I wanted to go up to Ari, but he met my sister's eyes, not mine, and then sat down without a word. I stayed where I was.

There was an embarrassing pause and then Ari's mother said, "You must be wondering why we are here. Arvind was discharged from hospital just this morning. He wanted to come and thank you. Well, we know how Arvind had got into a fight and…"

She was abruptly interrupted by her husband.

"I suggest we don't beat around the bush," he said. "This is not the first time we have had to deal with his wild behaviour. As a matter of fact, the last academic institution he attended, was forced to rusticate him. He beat up a teacher."

"The teacher was bullying a weak student," Ari's mother broke in. "Arvind has a very vulnerable heart. He is very altruistic."

Suddenly, Rhea got up, murmured something like an apology and left the room. Ari watched her leave, then flung his eyes down to the ground again. His parents continued to speak.

"So, what was he trying to do this time?" Ari's father rasped. He was clearly not waiting for an answer, but his wife broke in again. "He told me. He was protecting a boy who was being beaten up because he had a Muslim name."

She looked at my father and said, "Arvind told me your son was hurt too?" My father nodded. My mother said, "But not seriously."

Ari's father cleared his throat and began to speak. "We are beating around the bush again," he said. He turned to my grandfather. "Sir, my wife and I are medical doctors. I have specialized in tropical medicine and my wife is a gynaecologist. We together run a hospital for tribals in a remote area in Tamil Nadu. Since there are no academic facilities there, we sent Arvind to a prestigious residential school in a hill station. But look at what he does. He gets himself expelled just before his final term. So now he is a school dropout. A waste of eleven-and-a-half years of the best schooling in this country. My mother who lives here, is extremely distressed. We had to send Arvind to her, when the school insisted that he be removed. What else could we do? My mother moved to this colony less than a year ago. She lives a very retired life, she does not like to meet people. But that is not the issue. The police..."

His wife cut in quickly. Again.

"The police have been very kind," she said. "They assisted us in visiting the boy with whom Arvind had fought. He is recovering quite well. But the parents were really peculiar. They..."

This time, Ari's father interrupted her. It was as if the two of them were playing a game with each other.

"Peculiar?" he said with a snort. "They are religious bigots. The worst kind of human beings, Sir. They have taught that son of theirs to hate. To hate a certain community. Can anything be more evil? But we are beating around the bush again. We have to tell you that Arvind has…"

Ari's mother, however, had already got up and was saying, "We thought we should also look up this boy whose name created the whole problem. By the way, I believe the family is Hindu, so why was he called…"

It was my mother who answered. "His parents named him after their favourite playback singer, Mohammed Rafi," she said.

"Ah!" The two doctors spoke together for the first time. "That explains it." And Ari's mother added, "What a beautiful thing to have done."

All this time, neither my father nor my uncle spoke a word. Ari was totally silent, his eyes fixed to the ground. When his mother, then his father got up, he did too. So did all of us, except my grandfather who appeared not to have heard anything at all. I would have seen Ari to the front door, but for some reason, my father said, "Neel, please stay with your grandfather. I will see them out."

Ari's mother half smiled her thanks to everyone and led the way out. Her husband followed her, continuing to say, "We have just been beating around the bush. Just going round and round."

As they left the room, Ari suddenly turned to me and said, "Neel, I want to say…" Here he stopped, then went on, "About your grandmother. She was a gallant lady. And Neel…I am sorry. About, about everything."

He glanced up at the stairs, then turned and followed his parents out. That was the last time I saw Ari.

As they left, I kept wondering what it was that Ari's father wanted to say about his son. Why did he go on saying that they were "beating around the bush"? What beating around was it? What bush?

I should never have wanted to know this. Not for a thousand years. My stomach goes cold even now, when I think of what Inspector Khan told us an hour or so after Ari had left our house with his parents.

I wished then, and I wish now, that I never had to hear what he said. I never want to hear those words again. Never.

Ari was the ringleader of that gang of thieves. He was the organizer of the whole network, he was the paymaster, the boss, the brains behind the entire operation. My friend Ari. My only real friend.

"He told us he was bored," the Inspector said, talking to me as if we were alone, although the whole family was in the room with me.

"When he found how easy it was to enter an empty house like the Raj's place, he became more ambitious. You know how charismatic he is, Neel. You felt it." I nodded. I could not speak.

"He used that charisma very, very well, I'm afraid," the Inspector went on. "He convinced all those young, unemployed boys in the marketplace, that he would make them rich. He taught them football, he listened to their stories. He gifted them dreams. You know, Neel, not one of those young men would say a word against him, even after the whole thing came undone. It took us a long time to break their silence." He paused, then asked me, "Do you want to know how we finally found out?"

I nodded again.

The Inspector cleared his throat and said, "We found the little clock that used to be in the kitchen of the Doongaji sisters' house. We found it hidden among Pachamma's saris. When we confronted her with it, she broke down and confessed. But we still did not have the whole picture. We had to piece it all together, bit by bit."

The room was very quiet. My father spoke after a long time. "Arvind is a very mixed up person, Neel. You have to know this. You heard what about why he was expelled from school. You saw how he came headlong to fight with those boys who were attacking Rafi and you."

The Inspector added, "Do you know what he told us? He said he could not stand injustice."

I saw the fight again. I heard those poison words. I felt the blood in my mouth. In the quietness of our drawing room, in its safety. My sister covered her face with her hands.

I remember the silence in the room after he said this. The Inspector broke the silence. He said softly, almost tenderly, "Well, Arvind suddenly changed even while his plan was working pretty well. Pachamma, the other maids, Sundar, the young men were being paid with the proceeds of the stolen stuff. Apparently, Arvind kept nothing for himself. The only thing he did keep was that rare collection of music from the Bhonjo's place. Then suddenly, he called off the whole thing, as if he felt sick of what he was doing."

The Inspector paused. My sister ran out of the room, my mother followed her.

The Inspector waited a moment, then he said, "He dumped the stuff he could not sell as well as the cash he stole. He threw it into the fountain pool and made sure he was seen."

I found my voice. "You mean he was the ghost?" I asked.

"Yes, Neel," the Inspector replied. "He was the ghost gliding away on very well-oiled roller skates."

I remember how I sat there stunned, not able to speak. Then, little bits of scenes with Ari came back to me, and things that were mysterious stopped being mysteries. His bursts of temper, not talking about school, Pachamma rushing towards F block… It was like a jigsaw puzzle that I could fit together if I tried. But I didn't want to.

My father came to sit near me. He put his arm around my shoulders.

"It is hard, my son," he said softly. "I know it is. We kept it from you as long as we could. But it would have been cruel not to let you know."

"You knew?" I asked. "And you didn't tell me till now?" I asked. I remember I was almost shouting.

My father stayed calm, his arm was still on me. "Yes, Neel," he said. "We kept it from you for a little while. Your grandmother had passed away and you had your exams."

Yes, that was true. And yet, I wished…I don't know what I wished…I would not play football again.

"What will happen to him now?" I asked finally.

The Inspector replied, "He was produced before the Juvenile Justice Board and has been given bail. A special juvenile police unit will handle this from now on. The family has engaged a top notch lawyer. And he is trying to keep it away from the media."

The Inspector added, "The boy has to go through all the legal processes." I liked him for saying "the boy".

"You liked him, didn't you?" I asked. The Inspector nodded.

"We all did," my father said.

Suddenly, my grandfather who had not spoken for so many days, said, "He is a fine boy, Neel. And he is still your friend. His parents ought to have paid more attention to him, rather than attending to the rest of the world."

The Inspector left after shaking my hand as if I was as much a grownup as the others in the room. As my father and uncle saw him out, my grandfather held out his hand to me, "Come here, Neel," he said and hugged me when I went close to him.

"Remember, nobody is perfect," he said. "Not even a best friend."

Then he added in a gruff voice, "Your grandmother liked him very much too. She started calling him Dhruv."

Sitting in my room, on the bed, I tried to think of all that the Inspector had told me. I felt as if there were so many Aris. One Ari who helped me with my football and took time teaching me, another Ari who asked me not to drink cold water when I was all sweaty, a moody Ari chucking stones at a tree, another Ari charging up and butting that Sports fellow in the stomach.

Suddenly, it struck me that I had not asked the Inspector why Ari had changed so much that he threw away the things that were stolen. Including the cash. And he had done it in a very visible way. He had wanted to be seen.

What had changed him? A bad conscience? His grandmother? Something he had read?

My mother came into the room. She sat beside me and said, "Neel, darling. I have something more to tell you."

"About Ari?" I asked though I knew it would have to be about him.

"Yes," she replied. She hesitated before speaking again. She said, "It is difficult because…because I can't explain it myself. But here goes. You must be wondering why Ari changed so suddenly. Why he threw all those valuable things that were stolen. Why he made sure he was seen…"

I was wondering about that, I told my mother. "Why did he?" "He wanted to impress Rhea," my mother said and stopped.

I was thunderstruck. "Impress Rhea?" I asked. "Our Rhea?'

"Yes," my mother whispered. "He saw her for the first time when the three of us were coming out of the Doongaji sisters' house. Something seems to have happened to him then. He wanted desperately to be friends with her. He started following her. Almost chasing her. But…"

"But?"

"Rhea did not like him," my mother said quietly. "She was probably the only person, the only girl, he could not charm. The more he tried, the more she turned away. So then he began visiting us. And the rest of us fell under his spell."

"But Rhea…" I stammered. "Rhea is not yet thirteen. She is my younger…she is my little sister."

My mother hugged me then. "I know, Neel. But in such matters, age does not seem to be important. Ari saw something in her which none of us have seen. Something so beautiful that…"

She could not finish her thought.

"And," I said slowly. "She saw something in him that none of us did. Something not very beautiful."

My mother was silent. I was too. So we sat for a long time, as the voices of my father and my uncle floated up from downstairs, blending with the evening call of birds returning home to their nests, to their night's rest.

I wondered whether my mind would ever be able to rest again. My grandfather, my parents, my uncle, Rhea, all of us in this home had gone through such unrestful things in the past three months. So much confusion, pain. And Ari. What about Ari. What would he be thinking of?

My friend Ari. My best friend.

Then the doorbell rang, somebody opened the door, and Mrs Raj's voice bounded up like Dog. "Saach nice peepul," she was saying. "So good. So secoolar. Just like Mr Raj and myselph..."

My mother sighed and got up. "You'll be alright, Neel," she said. "So will Rhea."

I finish writing what I can remember of all that happened between January and March. I sit at my desk thinking of the burglaries, of the Banjo Club, of Twinkle, of Ari. Most of all I think of Ari, of friendship, of our friendship, his and mine.

Rhea comes into the room and asks me what I am thinking of.

"You look so serious, so old," she says with a laugh. "Like Grandfather."

I point to my diary and tell her about what I have written.

"May I read it?" she asks.

I hesitate for a moment, then give her the book.

She sits on the bed and reads without looking up even once. As she comes to a place somewhere near the end, she wipes her eyes and continues to read. When she finishes, she puts the book down, then gets up to give me a tight hug. "Oh Neel," she says softly. "How grown up you are."

But what is growing up, I wonder. I know now that it is not about being taller, or getting a moustache. "Do you know what growing up is, Rhea?"

She is silent for a while. Then she says, "I really don't know, Neel. I only know that growing up is higgledy piggledy."

And that is how I think I grew up. Between the start of January and the end of March this year.

In a higgledy-piggledy kind of way.

Just like my book. All mixed up.

THE END

Youngsters review the story...

I liked how the book was written accurately in the voice of a child. The quick change of thought, the curiosity and endless questions made Neel a likeable and relatable character, which is not common to see.

I found Neel's experiences with school especially amusing. The ups and downs he had through history class were very authentic and they made it easy for me to connect further with him.

I particularly liked the slightly historical and political elements about democracy and the freedom of India—especially how they were woven into the story rather than either being the main topic or not being there at all.

The plot line of the burglaries and Neel's family and school life all being intertwined with one another was what I liked most. Although the book started out very cheerful and light-hearted, the end was pretty shocking, with Neel's grandmother passing away and the situation with the police and Arvind protecting Rafi.

—Ameya Krishnaswamy, Student

Unexpected and frequent robberies suddenly take place in Neel's colony, as he and others hasten to find out what was going on. Nobody can be trusted as everybody seems to be having secrets of their own. Join him, as he attempts to find the criminal, while also grappling with getting older and the love he feels for his country.

Touching on almost all genres: action, thriller, comedy, drama and adventure, Mrs Poile Sengupta has produced another wonderful and thoroughly entertaining read for young adults.

—Aarjav Udani, Student

The story is very funny and shows the life of a young boy in a very humorous manner. It has a great plot. Poile Sengupta showed through everyday small ways how gender discrimination happens and how women are ignored in subtle ways. I would like to point out that in this book Neel is a very mature, developed character with a lot of depth. The one thing I might want to change about him is that he is seen talking about something very interesting, but the next minute he seems to be digressing. When he was telling us about a mystery that his (pesky) sister and Rafi were trying to solve, he stays on that point for some time but then goes on about what happened to him at school. I understand that Neel is the most developed character as it is written from his first person's view, but I would like to see more of some of the family members. As for Neel's friend Ari, the one that likes to play soccer with him, he has very frequent mood changes it seems, the type of a character that can be good and bad as a person. But, in the course of the story about the robberies in the neighbourhood, the readers would tend to think Ari as their prime suspect, as well as Neel's other friend, the "Tree Boy".

As a reader, I have to say the author is very good at creating drama and tension without exaggeration and convey the mass confusion and panic in Neel's neighbourhood without making the entire story centre around it.

Another thing I would like to change is for Neel and Rafi's relationship to improve profoundly after the incident where Rafi was bullied by other kids and beaten up.

At the end of the novel, Neel seems to have grown up in many unexpected ways. Some of the questions I would like to ask are who is Neel based on? How much research did you have to do about Gandhi and India's independence struggle? What made you incorporate Neel's low self-confidence in public speaking?

—Rohini Sinha Dasgupta, Student

About the Author

Poile Sengupta's work straddles five decades and all genres of writing. She is a playwright, poet, novelist and short fiction writer, both for children and adults. The sheer volume of her work for children is mindboggling—nearly two dozen books, and two dozen anthology entries. She has acted in the films *The Outhouse* and *Shaitan*. She was a member of the jury for the 2010 and 2012 Trinity Guildhall International Children's Playwriting Competitions, and for five years on the Governing Council of the National School of Drama, New Delhi.

ACKNOWLEDGEMENTS

Much gratitude to my editor Tina Narang, who has kept me cheerful through the process, and to Garima Syal, who helped shape the book. Also my thanks to Sanjoli C. for designing the endearing cover and to Stuti Sen for the lovely cover illustration. To Kamini Mahadevan for being my guiding star. Huge thanks to my young friends Ameya, Rohini and Aarjav for previewing the book.